Spiridon

Also adapted by Michael Shreve

John-Antoine Nau. *Enemy Force*

Spiridon

by
André Laurie

adapted into English by
Michael Shreve

A Black Coat Press Book

Acknowledgements: I should like to thank Paul Wessels for his generous and extensive help in the final preparation of this text.

English adaptation, Foreword Copyright © 2010 by Michael Shreve.
Cover illustration Copyright © 2010 by Jean-Félix Lyon.

Visit our website at www.blackcoatpress.com

ISBN 978-1-935558-61-3. First Printing. November 2010. Published by Black Coat Press, an imprint of Hollywood Comics.com, LLC, P.O. Box 17270, Encino, CA 91416. All rights reserved. Except for review purposes, no part of this book may be reproduced or transmitted in any form or by any means, electronic or mechanical, including photocopying, recording, or by any information storage and retrieval system, without permission in writing from the publisher. The stories and characters depicted in this novel are entirely fictional. Printed in the United States of America.

Introduction

In 2009, 100 years after its first and only publication,[1] *Spiridon* by André Laurie was awarded the Prix Nocturne, a literary prize given to the "dark suns of literature," i.e. imaginative or unusual works of fiction that have been forgotten or are out-of-print. It is difficult to imagine a more deserving recipient than this critically acclaimed work of science fiction, mystery, suspense, adventure story and social commentary. It is the final testament of André Laurie, a pseudonym of Paschal Grousset, who, like the novel, has been unjustly forgotten today.

Grousset was a prolific and multi-talented writer. He had an active career in journalism and during his lifetime he published more than 50 books under a number of pseudonyms, most commonly André Laurie and Philippe Daryl, but also Tiburce Moray, Léopold Virey, Docteur Flavius and others. In a way, the different names were used for his different forms of writing because he was a man of many facets and played a major role in various ways in the historic events of his day: militant journalist, communard sentenced to the penal colony, independent politician, energetic promoter of physical education, science fiction writer and "collaborator" with Jules Verne.

Paschal Grousset
Paschal Grousset's father was a math teacher from

---

[1] A new French edition was announced in 2008 by Des Barbares, but has not yet been made available to the public.

Grisolles in Tarn-et-Garonne in southwest France. He was posted in Corsica, where he became the principal of Collège Pascal Paoli and married Marie Catherine Benedetti, Grousset's mother. On April 7, 1844 Paschal Grousset was born and before he was two years old the family moved back to the paternal home in Grisolles. Despite his brief stay in Corsica, Grousset always kept a strong attachment to the island. The first time he ran for political office was as a representative of Corsica. He wasn't elected.[2]

In 1860 he went to Paris to attend school. When it was time for him to choose a career path, he decided on medicine and for four years pursued his studies. His interest in science continued throughout his life and influenced many of his different activities. Science alone, however, was not enough for him and he soon embarked on a new career in journalism.

In 1867 his writing debut took the form of a series of scientific chronicles that earned him a good reputation. However, living in the broiling times of the Second Empire amidst all the poverty and injustice in France, he was soon won over by republican ideas and was considered to be a socialist revolutionary even though he never admitted belonging to any group as he was fiercely individualist. He established his own paper as a young man, *La Revanche*, but it was short-lived. He also collaborated with *L'Epoque* and *L'Etendard*, a scientific journal, and then with *Le Temps* and *Le Figaro* under his own name and under the pseudonyms Dr Flavius and Léopold Virey.

For a couple of years he taught physiology and

---

[2] The "h" in his first name might well be a nod to the Corsican language.

anatomy at a girl's school in Paris, but driven to write, he began another career in literature alongside his journalism, and in 1869 published his first novel, *Le rêve d'un irréconciliable* (The Dream of a Diehard), a political work published under his own name. That same year he published *Madame de Léojac* under the name of Léopold Virey. He also published five historical works under his own name and another in collaboration with Jules Castagnary, Arthur Ranc and Francisque Sarcey.

1869 was also the year he began contributing to the columns of *La Marseillaise* (founded by Henri Rochefort), writing pro-revolutionary articles under the pseudonym Philippe Daryl. A little later he became the Editor-in-Chief. Grousset threw himself in headfirst. Being a firm opponent of the Second Empire and the imperial regime, he spoke vehemently about politics and refused to accept the unjust social and political conditions of the day. By the end of 1869, this caused one of the great scandals of the time.

Pierre-Napoleon Bonaparte, who was the cousin of Napoleon III, the Emperor, wrote a bitter and hostile article attacking *La Marseillaise*. Paschal Grousset felt personally slandered when Bonaparte wrote that he was going to end up "with his guts spilled out." On January 10, 1870 Grousset sent Ulric de Fonvielle and Victor Noir to the prince's home to demand satisfaction. The negotiations for the duel took a turn for the worse and Bonaparte shot and killed Victor Noir in the quarrel. The case went to court and Grousset, de Fonvielle and Henri Rochefort were convicted of an outrage against the Emperor and sentenced to six months in Sainte-Pélagie prison. Prince Bonaparte was acquitted, but had to pay damages. The funeral for Victor Noir took place on January 12 and somewhere between 100,000 and 200,000 angry people attended. It almost turned into a mass riot and the police were called to put it down with force. Some said that Rochefort missed an opportunity here to overthrow the government. At any rate, the obscure journalist, Paschal Grousset, was now a national hero.

On September 2, 1870 Napoleon III was defeated at Sedan and captured by the Prussians. The Third Republic was proclaimed on September 4, but the Franco-Prussian War was in full swing and the Germans were in control. When the five-month long Siege of Paris started, Grousset volunteered for the 18th Light Infantry Battalion and went to war. Within a few months, on January 28, 1871, France capitulated and signed an armistice. Grousset came back and two days later the Commune took effect on March 18, 1871.

The Paris Commune was a government of anarchists that is still seen by many today as a model of a free society. Basically it was a government of the working class, and Grousset participated in two, active ways. Firstly as a journalist: he established three successive newspapers, though none of them lasted long. Secondly as a member: he was elected for the 18th arrondissement of Paris and chosen as Delegate for External Affairs. Apparently he was not very successful at this post. His critics described him as "very external but with very few affairs." Of course, seeing that the Commune was surrounded by Republican troops at the time, "external affairs" was not worth much. Still, on April 12 he became a member of the Executive Committee.

Republican troops had been constantly assaulting the city and after two months the Commune was defeated in *la Semaine Sanglante*, The Bloody Week of May 21-28, during which tens of thousands of people were killed. After the fall of the Commune the government came down hard on tens of thousands more communards, sending them to prison, exiling them to New Caledonia or summarily executing them. Those who could, fled the country. Grousset refused to leave Paris and went into hiding. He was denounced, arrested, convicted by the Thiers government and deported to New Caledonia in June 1872. In March 1874, along with Henri Rochefort and a few others, he managed to escape from the island. He went to Australia, the Fiji Islands, San Francisco, New York and finally ended up in London, where he lived for six years.

In England he made a living teaching French and had a chance to observe English life up close which he put to good use when he started writing again. He left politics behind and under the name of Philippe Daryl he sent articles to *Le Temps* about student life and the educational system across the channel. Soon after these articles started appearing he got in touch with Pierre-Jules Hetzel to publish novels of his observations and study. At the same time he offered Hetzel some adventure stories which would lead to his "collaboration" with Jules Verne. But more on that later.

In 1880 a general amnesty was given to all communards (except for murderers and arsonists) and Grousset returned to France. Influenced by his English sojourn, he became a champion of physical education and for the next 12 years he led a successful awareness campaign for open-air sports and exercise, writing fervent articles and books promoting physical exercise in France. He continued writing novels, but eventually returned to politics. His first successful election was as an Independent Socialist Deputy for the 12th arrondissement of Paris in 1893, a position he held until his death.

As a Deputy he was busy on all fronts. He proposed

laws for the creation of pension funds to be managed by the Banque de France and promoted the rights of bicyclists. He wrote reports on freedom of election meetings, the establishment of income tax and the transportation of Diderot's ashes to the Pantheon. He voted in favor of the Separation of Church and State in 1905 and drafted several measures to help the needy. He is responsible for the electrification of a number of museums and libraries in Paris and for keeping them open late, whereby he hoped to bring culture to the people. On a more fanciful note, he proposed a laboratory for the fire at the center of the earth at the World Expo in 1900. It was his unforgettable "nail," a mile-deep hole that "clogged up" all the newspapers at the end of the year.

Throughout his political career, Grousset was deeply socialist, but he was not an internationalist or a Marxist or a communist. In fact, he kept his distance from all the various parties, factions and clans that make up the world of politics. His individualism and idealism are perhaps part of the reason for his obscurity today.

Philippe Daryl

Philippe Daryl was the name Paschal Grousset primarily used to promote physical education. In 1888 he created the *Ligue Nationale de l'éducation physique* (LNEP). It met with great success and the movement ended up organizing the first modern *Lendit*. A Lendit was the name of a fair held on an open plain between Paris and Saint-Denis in the Middle Ages where there were games and jousts. In 1889, the Lendit was revived and organized by Grousset as a series of physical contests for students in 12 events: bicycling, court tennis, discus, running, footrace, rowing, swimming, horse riding, high jump, fencing, shooting and French boxing. It was the official birth of school sports in France that aimed to reform all of French physical education.

The LNEP totally rejected competition in sport, considering it politically and morally harmful, as well as aristocratic. Grousset was always in favor of sport for physical health and overall well-being as an ideal of fraternization and popular education. He wanted to develop the abilities of the greatest number of participants, especially the weakest and those with the most difficulties, as opposed to the model that rewarded the smallest number of champions. This put him in complete opposition (both politically and in the very idea of sport) to Pierre de Coubertin. Coubertin inaugurated the first Olympic Games in 1896, an idea that Grousset had back in 1888. The two men spent years in conflict and hated each other. Coubertin was a militant aristocrat, conservative colonialist and anti-feminist and he refused to have any relations with Grousset and his democratic, egalitarian ideas that favored open-air, traditional sports for physical health and French cultural identity. Coubertin lived long enough to see and regret what would come of his ideals in the 1937 Olympics in Berlin. Grousset remained ever faithful to his own ideals, eventually establishing the Ecole Normale des Jeux Scolaires in the Bois de Boulogne where all the games of old France were revived, studied and practiced.

Philippe Daryl also published the first encyclopedia of sport, a four-volume work that appeared in 1892. Volume three was dedicated to ball games and was one of the main influences for bringing soccer into France.

André Laurie

In the end, however, Paschal Grousset's fame rests on the shoulders of André Laurie. As I mentioned,

Grousset pursued his literary career while in exile in London. In 1875 he contacted the editor Hetzel to offer a manuscript entitled *La métamorphose de Laurent Grivaud, Scènes de la vie de collège en Angleterre* (Schoolboy Days in England). The book was published in 1881 under the name of André Laurie and was a hit. It was translated into five languages and became the first in a series of 14 titled *La vie de collège dans tous les pays* (Schoolboy Days Around the World) between 1881 and 1904. The books had a great influence on public opinion about education in France as well as introducing different systems from foreign countries which allowed Grousset to express his progressive opinions about pedagogy, literature, science and culture. But it was his adventure stories that earned his legacy as one of the fathers of science fiction.

In the same year, Grousset sent Hetzel a manuscript of *L'Héritage de Langevol*. Hetzel did not like it much, but he bought the text with the idea of getting it rewritten by another writer. In this way, the pen of Jules Verne turned it into *Les 500 millions de la Bégum* (Begum's Fortune), published in 1879. A second manuscript suffered the same fate; *Le Diamant bleu*, which was written in 1880, became Verne's *L'Etoile du Sud* (The Southern Star Mystery) in 1884. Laurie legally renounced title to both the stories.

The third "collaboration" was on *L'Epave du Cynthia* (Salvage from the Cynthia) in 1885. Both authors' names appear on the text, although in their *The Complete Jules Verne Bibliography*, Volker Dehs, Zvi Har'El and Jean-Michel Margot deny any collaboration between Verne and Grousset, stating that Verne only did some "validation work" on Grousset's text, and that Hetzel added Verne's name as a co-author for marketing purposes. In fact the book, which was not part of the series *Voyages Extraordinaires*, was entirely Laurie's and Hetzel had finally come to recognize the quality of his writing.

André Laurie had a hard time as the "ghostwriter" of the star and it was a constant battle for him to be considered his equal. For his legacy too, this triple "collaboration" with Jules Verne was both a blessing and a curse. On the one hand, he might be even more obscure today if Verne enthusiasts hadn't continually dug up his name; on the other hand, his work might have been judged on its own merit rather than in the light of Verne's as it so often is today. But in the end, the shadow found its light and the student equaled the master.

André Laurie published over 20 books for Hetzel including the first French translation of R.L. Stevenson's *Treasure Island* in 1885 and two translations of Captain Mayne Reid.

Among his more remarkable novels is *Les Exilés de la Terre. Selene Company Limited*, published in 1887, which tells of an adventurous plan to exploit mineral resources on the Moon by pulling it closer to Earth. In 1888, *De New York à Brest en Sept Heures* (New York to Brest in Seven Hours), via Niagara Falls and a submarine collision, predicted a transatlantic tunnel. In 1890, *Le Secret du Mage* (The Secret of the Magician) discovered evidence of a scientifically advanced prehistoric society. *Le Rubis du Grand Lama* (The Ruby of the Great Lama) in 1894 featured a steam-powered flying island. *Atlantis* in 1895 described how the mythical land survived under a glass dome at the bottom of the sea near the Azores. *Le Géant de l'Azur* (The Giant of the Skies) in 1903 featured a revolutionary airplane and *Le*

Maître de l'Abîme (The Master of the Abyss) in 1905, a submarine.

And, of course, there is *Spiridon* in 1907, his last published work about a giant ant, gifted with great knowledge and an insatiable scientific curiosity but with no human feelings or emotions who becomes the victim of mankind's petty jealousies and fear of strangers: "Human stupidity and meanness always go farther than you would think." It is a dramatic departure from the influence of Verne.

Paschal Grousset got married in 1908 and died of kidney failure the following year on April 9, 1909, while serving his fourth consecutive term in office. He had just turned 65 and showed no signs of slowing down his multi-faceted and productive life. We can regret what he did not have time to do, but we must appreciate what he left behind. In all his efforts and battles, both in politics and literature, Paschal Grousset proved himself to be a visionary and offered an innovative insight into the world and his contemporaries.

Michael Shreve

Bibliography

Paschal Grousset

J. Castagnary, P. Grousset, A. Ranc, F. Sarcey. *Bilan de l'année 1868, politique, littéraire, dramatique, artistique et scientifique.* Paris, A. Le Chevalier, 1869
Le rêve d'un irréconciliable. Paris, Madre, 1869
La régence de Décembrostein. Paris, Madre, 1869
Les origines d'une dynastie, le coup d'Etat de brumaire an VIII. Paris, A. Le Chevalier, 1869
Les grands procès politiques - La conspiration du général Malet, d'après les documents authentiques. Paris, A. Le Chevalier, 1869
Le 26 octobre. Paris, Madre, 1869
P. Grousset, F. Jourde. *Quatre mille français en Océanie.* Not published as a book (in *Le Courrier de l'Europe*), 1874
P. Grousset, F. Jourde. *Les condamnés politiques en Nouvelle-Calédonie, récit de deux évadés.* Geneva, Imprimerie Ziegler, 1876
L'Affaire Dreyfus et ses ressorts secrets, précis historique. Paris, Société d'Editions Illustrées, 1899
L'Affaire Dreyfus, le mot de l'énigme. Paris, Stock, 1899

André Laurie
"La vie de collège"
La vie de collège en Angleterre. Paris, Hetzel, 1881
Mémoires d'un collégien. Un lycée de département. Paris, Hetzel, 1882
Une année de collège à Paris. Paris, Hetzel, 1883
Histoire d'un écolier hanovrien. Paris, Hetzel, 1884
Tito le Florentin. Paris, Hetzel, 1885
Autour d'un lycée japonais. Paris, Hetzel, 1886
Le bachelier de Séville. Paris, Hetzel, 1887

Mémoires d'un collégien russe. Paris, Hetzel, 1889
Axel Ebersen, le gradué d'Upsala. Paris, Hetzel, 1891
L'écolier d'Athènes. Paris, Hetzel, 1896
L'oncle de Chicago, moeurs scolaires en Amérique. Paris, Hetzel, 1898
A travers les universités de l'Orient. Le tour du globe d'un bachelier. Paris, Hetzel, 1901
L'escholier de la Sorbonne. Paris, Hetzel, 1903
Un semestre en Suisse. Paris, Hetzel, 1904

Adventure Novels

L'héritage de Langévol. Manuscript sold to Hetzel, 1878. Published as *Les 500 millions de la Begum*, by Jules Verne. Paris, Hetzel, 1879
Le diamant bleu. Manuscript sold to Hetzel, 1881. Published as *L'étoile du sud*, by Jules Verne. Paris, Hetzel, 1884
L'héritier de Robinson. Paris, Hetzel, 1884
L'épave du Cynthia. With Jules Verne. Paris, Hetzel, 1885
Le capitaine Trafalgar. Paris, Hetzel, 1886
Les Exilés de la Terre. Selene Company Limited. Paris, Hetzel, 1888
De New-York à Brest en sept heures. Paris, Hetzel, 1889
Le secret du mage. Paris, Hetzel, 1890
Le rubis du grand Lama. Paris, Hetzel, 1892
Atlantis. Paris, Hetzel, 1895
Un roman sur la planète Mars. Not published as a book (in *La revue Illustrée*). 1895
Gérard et Colette. Paris, Hetzel, 1897
Le filon de Gérard. Paris, Hetzel, 1900
Colette en Rhodésie. Paris, Hetzel, 1901
Le secret du volcan. Not published as a book (in *Le Globe-Trotter*), 1902-1903

Le toit du monde, aventures sur l'Himalaya. Not published as a book (in *Le Globe-Trotter*), 1903-1904
Le géant de l'azur. Paris, Hetzel, 1904
Le maître de l'abîme. Paris, Hetzel, 1905
L'obus invisible. Not published as a book (in *Le Globe-Trotter*), 1905
Paris à Tombouctou. Unpublished (submitted to Hetzel), 1905
Spiridon le muet. Paris, Jules Rouff, 1907

Translations and Adaptations
Le chef au bracelet d'or. Mayne Reid. Paris, Hetzel, 1881
La Terre-de-Feu, dernière œuvre de Mayne Reid. Mayne Reid. Paris, Hetzel, 1885
L'île au trésor. R. L. Stevenson. Paris, Hetzel, 1885

Philippe Daryl
"La vie partout"
La vie publique en Angleterre. Paris, Hetzel, 1884
Signe Meltroë, moeurs berlinoises. Paris, Hetzel, 1884 (novel)
En yacht, mœurs britanniques. Paris, Hetzel, 1885
Le monde chinois. Paris, Hetzel, 1885
Wassili Samarin. Paris, Hetzel, 1886 (novel)
La petite Lambton, scènes de la vie parisienne. Paris, Hetzel, 1886 (novel)
A Londres, notes d'un correspondant français. Paris, Hetzel, 1887
Les Anglais en Irlande. Paris, Hetzel, 1888
Renaissance physique. Paris, Hetzel, 1888

Encyclopedia of Sports
L'équitation moderne. Paris, May and Mottéroz, 1892

La vélocipédie pour tous. Paris, May and Mottéroz, 1892
Les jeux de balle et de ballon, football, paume, lawtennis. Paris, May and Mottéroz, 1894
Le sport de l'aviron. Paris, May and Mottéroz, 1895

Other writings
Récits de Grande-Bretagne et d'Irlande. Not published as a book (in *Le Temps*), 1877
The Picture Amateur's Handbook and Dictionary of Painters. London, Crosby Lockwood and Co, 1878
Le land Warrant, after Edward Eggleston. Not published as a book (in *Le Temps*), 1880
A Dictionary of Painters and Handbook for Picture Amateurs. London, Weales rudimentary series, 1883
L'aveu de Lilian. Not published as a book (in *Le Temps*), 1883 (novel)
Preface to C. G. Gordo, *Lettres de Gordon à sa soeur, écrites du Soudan.* Paris, Hetzel, 1884 (included in *La Vie Partout* in 1885)
Preface to E. Monin, *La santé par l'exercice et les agents physiques.* Paris, O. Doin, 1889
Preface to L. Ville, *La lutte française.* Paris, Librairie Mondaine, 1891
Histoire de deux enfants de Londres - Aventure nautique - Les bavardages de Fanny. Paris, Armand Colin, 1891
Le yacht. Histoire de la Navigation Maritime de Plaisance. Paris, May and Mottéroz, 1890

Tiburce Moray
Un ménage royal. Paris, Degorce-Cadot, 1882
Wassili Samarin. Published as a book under the pseudonym Philippe Daryl (in *Le Temps*). 1882-1883

Léopold Virey
Madame de Léojac. Paris, Bureaux du Figaro, 1869

SPIRIDON

I. A Housewarming Party

Doctor Aristide Cordat's housewarming party was a sensation among the artists and scholars of Paris. The socialites could not remember ever seeing such an entrance onto the social scene by a young man, fresh out of school. They had never seen such extravagance even from a renowned surgeon at the end of a successful career; never from a fashionable painter; never from the heir of a princely fortune ready to live life to the fullest for a couple of years. No one had ever shown such wild luxury or such a complete harmony of the refinements of art or paid such meticulous attention to all the conditions necessary for a doctor to guarantee the well being and safety of his patients.

It took place in a wonderful house on Avenue du Bois de Boulogne where a rich playwright once lived. It was located in the middle of a huge park and architects were hired to renovate and refurbish it from top to bottom. They were given strict orders that money was no obstacle and it did not take them long to accomplish their most demanding and ambitious work, not to mention their most extravagant.

The sitting rooms on the ground floor opened onto a magnificent greenhouse on one side and on the other side onto flowerbeds that stretched to the avenue. They were hung with royal tapestries and rare paintings and decorated with stylish furniture and marvelous contemporary sculptures. A monumental staircase led to the upper floors that everyone with good taste wanted to see, like they used to at the Opera. The study, library and laboratory were marvels of research and comfort. The operating room, which was paneled and covered with crystal, sparkled like a jewel in the soft light of the electric chandeliers. A bed with gauzy white sheets stood in the middle of the room under a huge bell. There were mysterious containers, tubes and coils that held an arsenal of liquid and gas poisons, artificial atmospheres, drugs and anesthesia of all colors—green, red, yellow, blue and opaline.

The guests got out of their cars under a vaulted entrance between two rows of white-liveried valets and entered the enchanted palace. The ultramodern setting was so new and impressive that when they saw and guessed its purpose they were overcome with astonishment, which turned into respect and, like it or not, reduced them to silence. But soon, as the sitting rooms filled up and opinions were whispered among them, the general impression that was gradually forming in their minds came babbling out in admiration and wonder.

"Have you seen the greenhouses?" someone asked.

"And the staircase?" another said.

"And the tapestries from Bruges?"

"And the wonderful Hobbema!"

"And the Watteau in the bedroom!"

"And the extraordinary little statues from Tanagra!"

"And the chemistry lab!"

"And the crystal hall!"

"Everything is perfect, stunning... How could this devil Cordat get together so many rare and priceless objects?"

"And the library! You just have to see it! He's got first editions, beautiful engravings and bindings like they don't make anymore."

"So what! When you pay for it…"

"So, Cordat killed the Mandarin?"

"What Mandarin?"

"I don't know, Voltaire's or Rousseau's…"

"For the start of his career, it's not so bad, at least! Because, you know, it was less than six months ago that we gave him the gold medal at school."

"Ah! We're living in times when it doesn't take years for a man to earn his value. Talk about people in a hurry!"

"Seriously, does he have a huge fortune?"

"Aristide Cordat? He hasn't got more than ten cents to his name as far as I know. His father was a good man, a farmer in Perche. He left him 60,000 francs or so that he honestly used up to finish his studies."

"I heard something strange, too. Last year after paying for his thesis to get printed, he only had 3000 or 4000 francs left. Anyone else would have used it to get set up in an apartment somewhere. Cordat didn't dream of it. He bought a second-hand little yacht and went off alone to cruise the seas. No one knew where!"

"It all makes sense. He shipwrecked on a gold mine!"

"You can laugh, monsieur, but you can't deny that it's very well possible and all this seems likely…"

"Humph! I don't believe much in gold mines. Anyway, I've never come across any that are profitable! It's true that I've bought some on the Stock Market, like anything else…"

"Quite so, gold mines aren't 'profitable' except when you sell them."

"Hold on, there's Morlet! Hey, my friend, Morlet, tell me, since you're a well-respected architect, how much would you say this palace is worth, everything included?"

"Everything included? Hmm…10 or 12 million, at the very least, and with no eye to profit. Figure it: two or three million for the land, the same for the construction, which is flawless, and for the furniture, which leaves nothing to be desired, and double it for the art, all first-rate."

"Really, you must be joking! Everyone knows that you get millions with only a few strokes of your drawing pen!"

"Oh! The pen still has nothing on the scalpel, monsieur, believe me, especially since it cannot be paid in advance and has started practicing *dichotomy*."

"Dichotomy? What kind of Greek sport is that?" a painter asked.

"The name that the gentlemen in the University give to the art of getting a reliable client simply by sharing his skin with the humble partner who introduced him."

"Is that done?"

"Much more than it should be! It's the best job for the bush-beaters of the profession. The dog who finds the chosen partridge only has to make him swallow the bitter pill of credit before the operation, which is deemed necessary and which "his glorious master never fails at. The poor partridge hesitates, then submits and it's a done deal. Instead of 100 *sous* for the visit the good apostle pockets 5000 or 6000 francs with no problem and no responsibility."

"Very clever. Too bad we don't do this in painting."

"Are you sure of that, my friend? Some awful skeptics say that few, if any, portraits or busts would ever be created without the kind help of middlemen."

"That's possible. But fortunately the commission is less costly than for the human butchers!"

"Oh! Hey! It's not like that! If we had to believe these wagging tongues, a square foot of oil painting would be easier to price, without all the brokers, than a bottle of Champagne..."

And the people were gossiping like this when a quartet of violins and cellos began playing on the second floor and everyone stopped talking. The music was exquisite and warmly appreciated. Dances started up at the sound of two orchestras that were hidden behind the flowerbeds in the big greenhouse.

Then a bell sounded and they dined at small tables in the basement that was converted into a "grill room." At the end of the party they had the cotillon. The formal ball was led by the Master of the House with the charming daughter of his illustrious teacher, Professor Falcimaigne, and was a big hit, even more so because it ushered in a new fashion: hanging from the ceiling were bunches of the most beautiful pearls and real diamonds...

And as the kind host led his dance partner around, he received enthusiastic thanks from the female company. He was a dashing young man, between 28 and 30 years old, graceful and strong in his custom-made suit, perfectly at ease in the brand new wealth. He surveyed everything with the calm, proud eyes of a man who was sure of himself.

Behind him appeared a mysterious person whom Aristide introduced to some friends. "Baron Tasimoura, my collaborator and in many respects my teacher! Don't be surprised by his silence, he still only speaks Tungus." And he added in the utmost seriousness, "But it will only take him six months to become a perfect Parisian."

And the Baron nodded his head very slightly to the curious crowd gathering around him. He certainly did not seem to be the least bit Parisian yet. He was short, with a huge head and his arms seemed to float in his tailored, loose-fitting black suit. The first surprise was his yellowish brown, waxy complexion that looked frozen like a mask under his stiff, bristle-like hair. And his slanting eyes looked blank until you suddenly felt like those two pale pupils pierced you to the marrow with their drilling stare. But almost right away he bowed, slapped his narrow chest with the top hat he held in his finely gloved hand and followed Aristide.

Then you could see that he limped in his tiny shoes or at least he did not hide very well his jerky, stumbling walk like a Chinese lady.

"I guess they tie the feet of both sexes among the Tungus," someone whispered.

"Among the Tungus! I think the gentleman seems more like one of Vaucanson's automatons!" Professor Merius retorted sharply as he watched him go away. "Didn't you see his emotionless face and wooden movements?"

"Excuse me, Professor," Doctor Cordat replied, who had just joined them and not heard but guessed the remark, "Baron Tasimoura is not an automaton and I will prove it to you very soon by some never before seen surgical operations that I intend to perform with his assistance, if you would do me the honor of accepting my invitation."

"It would be a pleasure, my dear Aristide. When?"

"Probably in four days. I'm in the process of getting a few rare or difficult cases from some hospitals that I'm counting on being treated here. And I can promise you some surprises."

"I'll look forward to it with great interest!"

In fact, not long after the memorable housewarming party, which was news all over Paris and beyond because the major newspapers of the world were wired the story and told about the marvels, a very different kind of party took place at the house on Avenue du Bois de Boulogne: three chosen subjects were brought from their respective hospitals to three separate rooms next to the "crystal hall." One of them had an aortic aneurysm, another was paralyzed in his optic nerve, and the third was confirmed with tuberculosis on the tops of his lungs. Each in his way was a lost cause. The invitations were addressed to six prominent physicians and two representatives from medical journals. The meeting was set for noon sharp and the total time planned for all three operations was 45 minutes.

The program was followed to the minute. At exactly midday six doctors' cars came one after another from the farthest corners of Paris and stopped before the front steps. They were followed by two modest carriages. Right away the spruced up men got out and quickly went up the monumental staircase and sat in the back cane chairs in the operating room.

Dressed from head to toe in long, white surgical gowns with white caps equipped with special goggles, Doctor Cordat and his collaborator were waiting for their guest in front of a gurney. As soon as the last guest took his seat, a glass bell was triggered and came down from the ceiling to cover the two surgeons. A partition slid into the wall and the first patient, asleep on a stretcher, was carried to the bed by two assistants. Two flexible nozzles came down from the ceiling and were attached to the sleeper's lips.

His chest, however, was bare and a few pinpricks in the skin proved that he felt absolutely nothing. Right away Doctor Cordat's silent collaborator, armed with strong scissors, went at the patient's chest. He made a swift circular incision and popped it open like he was opening a can of peanuts. Not a drop of blood shot out. The lungs were there, pink and healthy, rising and falling steadily.

Spreading the two lobes apart, Cordat exposed the arch of the aorta set in the heart, which was beating in its envelop with a constant but jerky rhythm. The purplish bulge of the aneurysm was sitting right where the arterial loop enters under the sac. Shapeless, thinned out and distended, the bulge looked ready to burst at every heartbeat. With a quick, firm grip Aristide Cordat squeezed the artery and put two strong clamps above and below the tumor, which he sliced off right away and threw in the pan of treated water. Then joining together the two gaping tubes of the aorta, he secured them end-to-end with four hooks that he coated with slimy adhesive and covered with a patch of sterile tissue. He took off the clamps, sprinkled a blue liquid over everything and then put back the chest cover blanketed with a cotton pad and said, "It's done. Bring in the next one!"

The operation had not lasted ten minutes. The young surgeon had them raise the glass bell and gave the pan to his professors who passed it around to verify the reality of the aneurysm, not without having some doubts about such a dangerous operation.

But the second patient had already taken the place of the first on the gurney, which was now set up straight like a chair. The two surgeons took their places on either side of the patient and lifted his sleeping eyelids. While Aristide was rolling the eyeballs in their sockets with the help of a tiny silver shovel, his collaborator drove the point of an electric pencil into the mucous membrane underneath to touch the optic nerve. There was a sizzling sound and a little puff of smoke. Then right away two rose water compresses were applied under a bandage and the stretcher was taken away.

"Next…"

The last was the tuberculosis. He looked like he was breathing his last breath and sleeping his final sleep. Under his dried up collarbones two lids had already been hastily cut away. Aristide Cordat lifted them up and bared the tops of the lungs. Two gray masses crisscrossed with streaks.

"Everything's ready and the curdy solidification that we started this morning is complete," the surgeon said. "There's not a drop of blood."

Armed with a big knife, he started slicing into the lungs like they were butter. In a few seconds the two tops were separated from the healthy parts and both were placed into the treated water. Antiseptic pads were quickly applied and the holes disappeared when he replaced the lids.

"Take him away and bandage him up in bed." Aristide said. He signaled them to lift the glass bell and he looked at his watch: 17 minutes, start to finish! "Messieurs, please take note that all three operations lasted 17 minutes!" he said to the witnesses.

"I'm stunned," the first one said as he got up. "Now it's just a matter of knowing how they will turn out."

"You can see for yourself whenever you want," the young surgeon replied, "because you know that from now on the three patients are entirely at your disposal to be examined at your leisure. But you have to give them time to wake up. If you'd like, we can all go and wait while having lunch."

A few witnesses of the memorable session could not stay—they had urgent appointments—and went down to the ground floor and left. The five that remained were Professors Falcimaigne and Merius, the two reporters and Joel Le Berquin, the hospital prosector and personal friend of Aristide Cordat. All of them were sincerely excited about what they just seen and obviously eager to know the details of the procedures that were put into practice.

"It's absolutely marvelous," Professor Falcimaigne said. "The downside is that the most serious operations are going to become so easy. You have ruined the profession, my dear friend."

"Not at all! I'm not the expert on the local anesthesia. I don't even know their details. They are the personal property of my collaborator, Baron Tasimoura."

"Okay. So, where is the Baron, then?"

"At the moment he is taking care of the patients using certain processes that only he knows and that I have no right to know until further notice."

"By God, he's going to have lunch, isn't he?"

"Never in public. He's very particular about that. Since he's used to eating rice with chopsticks, as is the custom in his country, he doesn't like to make a show during these feasts; at least that's what I imagine!"

"Don't you know his language?"

"Not too well. Only a few words."

"And that is what makes it hard to be curious! But it would be easy, I think, at least to get a rough idea by doing a chemical analysis of the liquids and gases that he uses!"

"I have given my word not to examine them and it's only under this condition that I have been able to show you some results."

"Damn! What a secretive fellow! He has to know that without knowing how the anesthesia works the whole thing falls apart. How can we even talk about these operations to the Academy of Medicine or any organization of surgeons? It will sound like magic!"

"It doesn't matter, if the effect is positive and irrefutable."

The coffee had just been served when Baron Tasimoura's silhouette appeared in the doorway of the dining room. Aristide got up, went into the next room and took his associate's hand like he was feeling for a pulse. After a minute he came back to his guests.

"The patients have regained consciousness and are at your disposal, gentlemen. But if you'd like, we can first take some time to smoke a cigar."

Twenty minutes later all the guests were on the upper floor conducting a detailed exam of the patients in their separate rooms. Not only were the three patients in perfect possession of all their faculties, but they also seemed to be in perfect health and were heartily eating the meal that was served to them. Not one of them had a fever or felt uneasy. They willingly allowed their surgical wounds to be examined, which were already in full recovery and almost scarred.

The two professors could not get over it and the reporters faithfully noted down their admiration.

But Joel Le Berquin did not say a word. He felt, smelled and tasted everything like a man determined to found out the secret of these miracles. After the others had gone their separate ways, he stayed behind to smoke a pipe in Aristide's office. He was obviously hoping to pry some private information out of his friend.

But Aristide was in a good mood and remained inscrutable.

"Don't press me, my friend, I can't say anything for the moment because I barely know any more than you about the composition of the precious anesthesia that you saw us use. Maybe someday I'll know more. Anyway, I hope so and then you can be sure that you will be among the first to find out. For now, you've seen and appreciated everything I can possibly show to the public."

Joel Le Berquin had to be satisfied with this statement. He finally said goodbye to his friend and walked down the avenue to the Latin Quarter.

II. The Case of Monsieur Baselli

The author of this true story here is not sworn to the same strict secrecy as Aristide Cordat and can backtrack and make a short review of the events that led up to the triumphant debut of the young surgeon in the good city of Paris.

On the day after his last doctoral exam and after paying off all his bills, Aristide Cordat, as we have seen, found himself with a few thousand francs and a little yacht, La Mouette, which he had bought in Gennevilliers. The season was ripe for a nice voyage on the sea. Aristide's mother was originally from Nice and he had always promised himself to visit the western islands of the Mediterranean, the Balearic Islands, Corsica, Sardinia and Sicily. He figured he would never have a better opportunity, so he had his yacht brought to the station in Lyon and by train to Toulon for the necessary preparations. He himself took a fast train to Marseille a few days later and soon met up with his boat to start his planned cruise. His friend Le Berquin was supposed to go with him, but he had to cancel at the last minute. So Aristide left with a young ship's apprentice as his entire crew.

First he visited Calvi, Ajaccio, the strait of Bonifacio and the naval base in La Maddalena where the Italian authorities turned out to be very suspicious of his purpose. On the west coast of Sardinia, he was caught in a wind storm that made the yacht almost uncontrollable after his young ship's apprentice was swept overboard, carried away like a feather by a ground swell.

For six hours the young doctor fought desperately against the elements, but he could not enter the Gulf of Terranova. Suddenly to his right he saw a dark cove and headed toward it with great patience and effort, going against the wind the whole way. Not only was the sea relatively calm there, protected by the high, steep cliffs to the south, but the cove seemed to lead into an underground river through a deep grotto sheltered at the foot of a cliff.

Some traces left on the rock showed that at certain times the river must have turned into an angry torrent rushing down from the nearby mountains and swollen suddenly by rains and a hundred stormy creeks. Now it was almost dried up and the only thing the sailor could do was to put up in dead water right before the entrance to the grotto. He got off the boat right away, hoping to explore the bay and find a town or at least a village where he could get fresh supplies for himself and his yacht. But the cove was deserted and wreckage left on the shore by the storm showed clearly enough that it was not inhabited because it was inhabitable.

Aristide took stock of the situation and decided to climb the rocks that overhung the cove to the east so that he could scout out the surroundings and look for a way to get some much-needed help. So, he took his shotgun from the yacht, along with some ammunition and food, and set off.

He had not gone up 100 yards when he was sure of one thing: the coast was absolutely deserted for two or three leagues around and difficult to get to from any direction other than the sea. But he also noticed that on the side of the next range of mountains there were some crops that looked like vines and in places some black specks that could have been huts, if not houses.

Getting his bearings carefully, he chose the direction that seemed easiest and got on his way. For a long time he climbed through rocky lands where there were only golden-chain and strawberry trees and now and then a patch of green. The sun had disappeared behind the western heights and the night was slowly coming on when the tired tourist saw to his right, at the bottom of a dark little valley, a fire that might indicate a dwelling. A few minutes later he could tell that the light meant human beings. It was a poor hamlet with five or six clay huts. He naturally chose the one with the light. The door was open and he went inside.

A rather pretty young woman was busy cleaning while a full-bearded man was fixing a fishing net that hung from the black crossbeams of the ceiling. The fire that the traveler had seen from afar burned in a hearth made of rough stone in the middle of the room and the smoke rose up to the roof that was made of open-work slats through which the starry sky shone.

Even though the visit of a stranger was maybe an unprecedented event in this place lost on the western edge of the island, neither the father nor the girl showed any surprise. They seemed sad and preoccupied by some bitter care.

"*Salute*," the doctor said in the doorway.

"*Salute a Vossignoria!*" the man and his daughter answered without stopping their work.

Aristide told them how he had got there and that he had left his boat in the grotto on the coast at the foot of a mountain. And in his best Italian of Nice, he explained that he needed two or three experienced workers to fix his boat.

"Workers! You won't find them here. You'll have to go find them in Gonargientu," the fisherman explained.

"Is it far from here?"

"Thirty miles or so," the man said and added, "if only Orso was still here, the two of us might be able to take care of it..." He sounded like he was weighed under some sorrowful, obsessive thought. "But he disappeared three weeks ago."

"Your son, I guess?" the doctor asked sympathetically.

"Yes, *Signor*. The best and most beautiful boy on the coast," the poor man replied. "He went looking for a goat in the Nurri valley and never came back." The memory was so painful to his daughter that she broke out in tears with the boilerplate in her hands.

"And what is this valley?" the traveler kindly asked to take their minds off such bitter grief.

"It's a cursed valley that goes down to the sea on the other side of the mountain. Whoever sets foot in it never comes back! Orso didn't believe the stories and he went there and now we cry over him."

The young woman's grief became so intense that she jumped up and left to smother it somewhere else.

"I'm sorry that I accidentally brought up such a bad memory," the visitor answered. "But what's so dangerous about this valley? Bad air—*aria cattiva*; fevers?"

"No one can say. No weeds grow there. No living being is there. Everyone avoids it. But the true and certain, undeniable fact is that whoever sets foot in it disappears and never comes back...we always heard about it...Orso didn't want to believe it and now he's gone..."

"It should be cleared up. Maybe there's a source of the evil," the doctor said. "If you would like to go to

Gonargientu tomorrow to look for a couple of good workers, I can see to investigating the problem while you're gone. I'm sure we will find that there's a very simple solution and a natural explanation to your son's disappearance."

"I will gladly go to Gonargientu to hire the necessary workers. But believe me, *Signor*, drop the idea of going out there. It will cost you your life."

"It's okay. It's not the first time that I've cleared up a matter!" the other tossed out. "In matters of mystery, my good man, you always have to go to the very depths...and you usually find the simplest explanations." Aristide took some gold pieces out of his hunting belt and put them on the table. "Here's something you can take to town to bring back the best workers you can find. And in the meantime if you could give me something to eat, I would be very grateful because I'm starving."

"I'm sorry, but we don't have a lot in our humble home. Some bacon, a few eggs, a little bruccio maybe... Pia!" the fisherman called, tantalized by the sight of the gold that looked like a huge, unheard of amount to him. "Set the table for the gentleman. We have to cook up a little something for him to eat."

The young woman came back in and silently started doing what her father had asked. Soon the tablecloth was laid out and bacon was sizzling in the pan, eggs turned into omelets and a bottle of Lambrusca wine, probably the only one, was dug out of the bottom of the cupboard. It is the nectar that the Sardinian peasants get from the meager vines of wild Muscat that cling to some of their rocks. Finally the *bruccio*[3] was served, still warm in its

---

[3] Goat milk cheese.

wicker basket, on a brown earthenware plate. Instead of bread they served a big slice of polenta.

The traveler sat at the table with the father and daughter. He went at the rustic food with an appetite sharpened by the country air and by the long day. Everything was delicious to him. His good mood ended up making his hosts forget their troubles. They felt so much better that when Baselli saw him lighting his pipe with a hot coal he said that he would go to his neighbor or to his partner Susinu to find a bottle of old Grappa that they would surely give him. And he left to negotiate the important business.

He came back pretty soon with the partner he mentioned and a bottle of grape-skin alcohol and both of them started talking about their adventures. They had sailed together, seen the Red Sea, Abyssinia and even the Battle of Adowa. They also worked together in the naval base in La Maddalena for long enough to earn the money for a fishing boat that they bought together and at the moment was being rented off the coast of Tunisia.

Their travel stories ended up making the doctor sleepy. He was happy to throw himself on a bed of dried grass that Pia, who had kept busy and quiet, set up for him in the corner.

When he woke up the next morning he found a basin of fresh water on the table, some white towels and a bowl of milk. He washed up the best he could, swallowed the milk and went out.

By the time he was in the doorway Pia was already chatting. She was sitting in the shade of a fig tree and dressed so unexpectedly that the doctor stood there dazed. She was wearing a blue velvet blouse with tight sleeves buttoned from the wrist to the elbow with little bells, a wimple, a red skirt with small pleats, trimmed with blue satin and silver stitching, heeled stockings, buckled shoes and her hair was held up in a purplish-red cap.

"My dear Pia, you look very beautiful this morning in your courtly dress," he said smiling.

"It's my formal dress that I only put on for very special occasions," the young woman answered solemnly. "And what occasion is more special than a visitor like you, *Signor*, who wants to go looking for my brother!"

"Has your father left?"

"This morning at the break of day. He hopes to be in Gonargientu before noon and bring back the workers you need this evening."

"Perfect. As for me, I'm going to take a look at the Nurri valley, as we agreed. Is it far from here?"

"Toward the sea, over that mountain," she pointed to the southeast.

"That's the same direction I came from when I left my boat."

"I would come with you," the young woman admitted, "but my father strictly forbade me to leave."

"And rightly so. Your place is here and nowhere else. Do you think I should bring some provisions?"

"Of course. And I've prepared them. I have some hard-boiled eggs, dried figs, a piece of polenta and a flask of old wine."

"All's for the best...I'll take my gun and go!" Aristide Cordat went into the house, checked his shotgun, buckled his shoes and came out again. Pia handed him the flask and the cloth sack that she had prepared.

"Goodbye and thank you, dear friend," he said holding out his hand.

"It's me who should thank you and bless you from the bottom of my heart!" she answered kissing his hand.

"Goodbye, *Signor*. Happy hunting for some good clues. It's this way," and she pointed out a path to the right. Her lips were trembling and her eyes were misty.

"See you this evening!"

He went away and the young woman followed him with her eyes to the top of the mountain.

Eight a.m. was sounding from an unseen clock when the doctor got over the ridge to the next valley and bounded down the slope. Beyond the mountain the land stretched out in waves just like the day before and the terrain to the southeast pointed out by the course of the sun was in stark contrast with the green land he had just left. The few plants became more and more sparse and the folds of land dragged on forever. The wind coming from the sea beyond the horizon swept over the shallow craters that were formed there. Aristide walked for a long time, three or four hours, without seeing anything of interest or anything that particularly attracted his attention. Crater upon crater was spaced out one after another; deserted land followed upon deserted land; and not a single living being livened up the solitude. He was just about to give up the useless march to the sea when suddenly, as he climbed over a block of stone that was barring the way, he saw at a distance, on the edge of the horizon, the straight gray line of an old tower. The sight put some energy back into him. He sped up and quickly crossed the expanse that separated him from his goal.

When he got to the foot of the tower he was not surprised to notice that it was in ruins and looked abandoned. The walls rose straight up to the sky with no windows or openings of any kind except a few arrow slits cut between the huge blocks of granite that the four faces were made of. At the top of the cyclopean walls the crenellations had withstood the force of the winds, rains and centuries, but behind them you could imagine a chasm of hundreds of square feet formed by the collapse of the floors between the unshakeable rock of the walls. The impression was made stronger by the 100-year old trees that were growing on high, which had no doubt sprouted from the crevices in the granite and were turning green again on the top of the tower after being burnt by lightening.

Aristide walked all the way around the trench that was probably an ancient pit, but he found no trace of any door or drawbridge. Some V-shaped iron bars that remained in place a little off the ground seemed to suggest that there were once some auxiliary constructions to the donjon that probably led outside by some underground route and that were now the only remnants of what could have been a powerful fortress.

On the sea side the tower stood on the rock itself, a little distance from the sheer cliff that plunged into the sea. The face of the cliff made the doctor think that he was exactly above the underground river where he had sheltered his boat the day before. He swore to himself to check it out when he had time, thinking that without even trying he had probably discovered one of the prehistoric towers they call Phoenician, which are not too rare on the coast of Sardinia. In Gaelic they call these towers "nurraghs": ancient lighthouses for sailors of old that were no doubt also refuges and forts that they took great care of. All this deserved a few hours of study one of these days.

But for now he felt tired and hungry. He decided to take a break and have lunch in the shade, so he went back to the north side of the tower where there were some thin bushes. He sat in the weeds in the part of the pit that was sheltered from the sun, took the frugal meal out of his bag that his host's daughter had prepared and started eating heartily and drinking the old wine from the flask.

While he was busy at this he felt a few drops fall on his face and hands that he thought was seaspray carried by the wind, even though the clear sky told otherwise. Moreover, the drops smelled musky, which surprised him, and so he intended to look for the cause.

But his thoughts did not go much further. At the same time as this kind of scented dew hit him, he felt drowsy and kind of numb. His head fell back and his body followed. He put up no fight and dropped into the weeds.

The last thing he remembered was that as he fell asleep he breathed in a strange aroma close to his face that he thought came from the wild plants where he lay down.

3. The Anatomist

When Aristide regained consciousness and opened his eyes, he found himself in a large, vaulted room that he had never seen before and that was lit up by electric light bulbs.

It took him a little time to realize what had happened as he stared at one of the blinding bulbs above his head. At first he thought he was lying on a bed that felt very hard. This surprised him. He wanted to be sure and tried to get up on one elbow, but he could not do it.

Then he got the idea that he was tied down flat on a marble table. And this was confirmed by the cold that his hands felt where they were lying.

But his neck was free and he could turn his head, with difficulty, to the right and left. His head felt very heavy. He tried desperately to understand and see and finally decided that the back of his neck was lying on a block of wood.

Almost at the same time his eyes fell upon an object not far from him that he first thought was a man sleeping. But it was something completely different, as he found out when he turned his head a little farther. A corpse, *dorsal decubitus*, with a gaping abdominal incision! The lungs, heart, liver and intestines of the corpse had been taken out and placed in jars filled with water and alcohol on the marble table where it lay.

Even though he was used to such sights as this, the doctor was struck with horror and amazement. The table where the slaughter was spread out was parallel to his and maybe six feet away. Was he himself being kept for the same purpose? They obviously thought he was dead if they put him in an anatomy laboratory and such a place clearly showed what they wanted to do with his mortal remains.

Dead—he certainly was not. He felt his heart beating in his chest, his arteries pulsing through his limbs and brain, his lungs breathing in and out; he even felt the hair on his head standing on end because of the terrible danger that he had just gone through. And the danger was not over yet, surely. Wasn't he paralyzed in three fourths of his body and unable to get up on the slab? And what if he was going to fall back into unconsciousness and become lethargic like he was just a minute ago? What if the anatomists who had torn his neighbor to pieces found him senseless and still, were they going to get to work, open up his belly and chest, take out his insides and put them in jars?

The thought of it was so frightening that it had exactly the effect that he so feared: Aristide screamed and called for help, which did not come, and for a second time he passed out.

How long did this second unconsciousness last? He could not say. He snapped out of it when he felt a stinging pain in his left arm and he knew that his ghastly nightmare had become reality.

An unrecognizable man was there, sitting on a stool next to the table and starting to dissect his arm, Aristide's arm! There was a large incision down the middle of his arm from the shoulder to the wrist and the skin was pulled back by dissection hooks, as thin as fishhooks, with little chains, which were hooked onto the other end to his still intact chest. The blood flowing from the long wound was soaked up by thin sponges; the muscles were separated from each other and in plain sight; metal rods held apart the veins and arteries from the thin, white nerves that ran the length...

At this awful sight, barely glimpsed, Doctor Cordat howled in protest. He cried out that he was not dead, that there was a tragic mistake and that he had to stop that very second.

But the anatomist kept working, unconcerned, as if he had not heard him wailing. He lifted up a muscle with some tweezers, carefully took off some connective tissue or some fatty tissue and placed it gently on the marble. At times he referred to an engraving in the Italian book that was open on the patient's belly.

Just then Aristide noticed that he felt no physical pain and barely even felt the touch of the scalpel in the thick of his skin. He understood that the sharp pain that woke him up was due to the incision in his skin and thinking wholly on a professional level he started taking a keen interest in the operation that was being performed on his body.

"I would have thought my biceps were more developed!" he said kind of bitterly. "That's what happens when you only practice fencing and you trade in the good rowboat of old for an electric motor! I sure hope that my right arm is a little more muscular than that! Why did this creep choose the left arm?"

From the anatomical preparation that he was already watching with a philosophical eye, he naturally turned his attention to the torturer who was dissecting him.

He had a medium build, was wearing a white cotton sheet and seemed strangely agile and muscular under his shapeless smock. His bulky head was covered with a kind of hood, also made of white cotton, and where the eyes should have been a pair of glasses glimmered, or more precisely, glass was set into the fabric. But what really drew the patient's attention were the hands that poked out of the operator's big sleeves and, to tell the truth, looked a lot more like crab claws than hands so to speak. Imagine a kind of toothed, horny claw, totally black, with a kind of thumb and prehensile part but no other secondary fingers. The patient being dissected alive gawked at them.

It did not take long to see that the anatomist used them with exceptional skill and that the thumb, which was covered with a very smooth skin on the inside, would sometimes glide over the details under study and touch a part here or there, as if it were painstakingly filling in some information.

This observation seemed so interesting to the young doctor that he forgot all about the rest and almost automatically tried to move his free arm and grab the paw of the creature carving him up. He managed to do it because either the anesthesia in his free arm had worn off or his will power had triumphed over his paralysis.

A second later Aristide's right hand fell upon the operator and grabbed his thumb, making him drop the scalpel.

The anatomist suddenly stopped what he was doing, pointed his glasses down to the patient and looked deeply surprised that he was still alive.

The strange thing was that while Aristide was holding onto the medical student's thumb with his fingers this surprise was literally translated to him by a series of long and short electric shocks that went from the thumb to his hand and were translated into perfect Italian like they were some kind of mental Morse code:

"Hold it! Hold it! The stiff's not dead! How lucky I am to carry out my study on the living! I'll take advantage of it, do what I can to keep him in such a useful state and verify this idiot's peristaltic movements of the stomach, the interelementary circulation, *ed oltre cose bellisme!*"

And then the monster pulled free of his victim's grip and went to get a strap from the cabinet. He tied down Aristide's right arm to hold it firmly against the dissection table. After taking out the hooks and other tools that were holding back the muscles and vessels of the dissected limb, he very skillfully replaced every organ in its normal position and bathed the whole thing in a blue liquid using a thin sponge. Then he simply closed up the skin with the hooks, sprinkled the same blue liquid over it and lastly wrapped the wound in a cotton bandage. When this was done he put the bottle in its place on the shelf and came back to the strapped down patient. He quickly thrust a little glass tube full of a colorless potion into the patient's mouth and right away poured it down his throat. The patient swallowed it gladly because he was dying of thirst.

With the matter settled like that, he went out, closed the door and left the victim to his thoughts. There were not many; the doctor was already asleep.

When Aristide had finished his nap and woken up by himself, he could tell, in the first place, that he was in good health and that he felt only a little stiffness in his dissected arm. Afterward he knew that the paralysis was definitely over and he had free use of his limbs, if it wasn't for the leather straps across his right arm and chest binding them to the marble table. How was he going to undo these straps?

The young doctor looked around the tragic cellar where his torture was unfolding, but he saw no way to free himself.

To his right the corpse was still there lying on the table, gaping at the unknown above the jars holding his entrails. To his left two other empty tables were waiting for subjects.

In front of him the half-open cabinets revealed their collection of multi-colored bottles, pans, and surgical tools. Some clothes were hanging from a hook and Aristide recognized them: his hunting jacket, his leather belt, his felt hat and just next to them his gun...

The pressing need to lay his hands on the weapon made him shudder on his bed of pain. Oh! If he could just get on his feet with the gun in his hands! He would waste no time sweeping away everything in front of him and getting rid of all obstacles to see the blue sky again. But it was impossible under that crushing grip of the cursed strap.

And suddenly as this thought was blazing in his feverish head, his left arm, his dissected arm moved to the edge of the slab and he felt something cold under his hand. He grabbed it in anger.

The scalpel! It was the scalpel that had fallen out of the anatomist's grip when he was interrupted in his macabre task.

He only needed this to free himself and it would take just a few minutes. Putting all his energy into his wounded arm, Aristide managed to bring the blade of the scalpel up to the strap that was holding him down. He sawed at it, or rather wore it down with the blade and after a heroic effort, cut through! He was free!

He jumped to his feet, got dressed and grabbed his gun and belt. It all took him less than a minute. The door was not locked, it opened easily. A second later and Aristide went through and closed it again. He was in a long hallway lit by electric lights as far as the eye could see.

A brighter light on the right attracted his attention. He went that way and came to a vast gallery that was really a large wheat field ready for harvest, growing under cover of the intersecting fires of thousands of lamps.

At first Doctor Cordat was stunned by the sight stretching out before him, but soon he had to face the facts. Not only was the magnificent wheat growing in the very ground of the cellar, but it was ready for harvest and there were millions and millions of ants calmly getting on with the job! Grain by grain they shucked the wheat right on the stalk, heaved up their booty and tumbled down to the ground. Then they took their place in the single file of their fellow ants and carried their load away as fast as they had got it.

Where were they going? Were they carrying their crop to some mysterious granary? Aristide did not dream of asking them. Completely surprised by the sight unfolding before him, he only snapped out of it when he noticed that some well-managed streams were watering the wheat field on all sides. The streams were coming from tanks made of large stones in the corners of the gallery and looked like they were flowing into other reservoirs set up under the ground, which was clearly made of sand and chemical fertilizer. Everything was very well organized and very well taken care of, not to say very refined.

The clearness and freshness of the murmuring streams awoke in Aristide two feelings that he was eager to sate: hunger and thirst. After quenching his thirst in the nearest stream, he gathered a handful of ears of wheat, rolled them in his hands to shuck them and ate.

The puffy grain was wonderful, so soft and mouthwatering that the most skillful baker could not have made them tastier. Aristide took seven or eight more handfuls without worrying about what the ants might think of his craving. In fact, they did not seem to be paying any attention to him. They were completely absorbed in the work they were doing devotedly. As far as the taster, he already felt energized with a new will and vitality, as if the grains of wheat, scientifically cultivated in a totally artificial environment, contained and combined the principles of health and strength.

He was curious enough to follow the ants to see where their granaries were and soon he came to a series of vaulted storerooms where the wheat was heaped up in large, ordered piles. However, some of the workers, instead of bringing their fresh grain to one of the growing piles, seemed to have another goal and left the line to go to a gallery farther away. Aristide followed them to a nursery full of newborn larvae. Nursing ants fed them the fresh grains, putting them directly into their mouths after first crushing them with their mandibles. While the infants were greedily munching their food, the nurses continued their mother's work by licking the larvae with the greatest care to get rid of any impurities that might have got on them while they were unconscious. The larvae looked like they fully appreciated this meticulous care because they did not budge an inch while it was happening, except for their chewing. Aristide Cordat was quite struck by the fact that his presence did not seem to bother the nurses in the least, or better said, they paid no attention to him.

He left after that to continue exploring the galleries and visiting one wheat field after another in different stages of growth. Some were just starting to grow, while others were more advanced or even ready for harvest; still others were just planted. But order and regularity reigned everywhere—a phalanstery solely occupied with the common good.

The visitor really wanted to investigate the dark regions of this social organization that was obviously expanded underground through small secondary openings at certain points where the workers disappeared in single file. But he did not even think about it without special equipment like those transportable windows for ventilation that you see sometimes in agricultural exhibitions. And after an hour of these basic observations Doctor Cordat went back to his voyage of discovery with the secret hope of finding the home of the anatomist who had been working on his body.

But in this hope he was disappointed. After a careful exploration of the electrical system that ran along the sides of the underground hallway, he had to admit that his search was in vain and he was just about to give it up when he noticed a very gradual slope at the end of a deserted gallery.

At first glance, the ramp reminded him a lot of the one he had seen once in the famous Moorish tower in Seville, the Giralda, which lead up, floor by floor, to the top of the tower. Supposing that the primitive elevator could end up at a floor where he might meet someone of a higher species who surely ruled over the Myrmidon ant people, he set off determinedly on the paved slope.

To tell the truth, he was nervous and emotional. His heart beat fast and his hands gripped the gun as he took the first steps that might prove decisive. But here again his expectations were let down. The ramp led to a dark gallery that had obviously been abandoned long ago, maybe centuries before. A faint light from the outside filtered through two or three arrow slots cut into the wall. The gallery contained nothing but long rows of unfired bricks and piles of clay balls. Everything was covered with a thick layer of dust.

What could have been the purpose of these bricks and balls? Aristide was curious to find out. He cleared away two or three to bring them out and examine them in the light of the hallway.

When he first lifted them up, he was surprised by the heavy weight of the objects, which did not seem to fit at all with their size or appearance. The bricks and balls might as well have been made of lead, which would have been no more difficult to handle.

With his left hand pretty useless because he was carrying his gun, the best he could do was to get one specimen of each kind and go back down into the light with his findings. When he got back into the hallway, he dropped them on the ground, with no other purpose than to get rid of the awkward weight. And the brick broke right away…

It held an ingot of fine gold that under the harsh light of the electric globes looked as brilliant as on the day long ago when it came out of smelting and was wrapped in its clay mold.

Aristide spontaneously picked up the clay ball that had rolled away and threw it on the ground. It broke like thin bark and under its skin was a diamond as big as an egg, cut into sparkling facets!

Aristide was speechless before this unexpected sight. Leaving his precious shards on the ground, he marched back up the ramp, grabbed another brick and ball at random in the deserted gallery and broke them against the rock wall. In both the results was the same: a gold ingot and this time a huge sapphire shined before his eyes, flashing their light in the semi-obscurity of the room.

There could not be the slightest doubt. A priceless treasure slept in the dust of this gallery, which was maybe not the only one of its kind in the colossal ruins where the fortune had been stored. The distinctive features that struck the young doctor when he got to the old tower came back to mind. He told himself that the prehistoric building was no doubt an ancient Phoenician establishment from long ago where the brave sailors came, maybe through underground passages, to dump their Asian and African loot. Many generations of pirates piled up all their treasure of fine gold and precious stones on this wild land of Sardinia, on the shore of the sea that had been their highway. Then they disappeared or were shipwrecked, carrying their secret to the tomb and the treasure remained with no one to claim it. Revolutions and catastrophes had passed over them. Winds and storms and centuries had hammered away at the Phoenician fortress and slowly brought it to ruin, burying its history in the mists of the past. The Carthaginians, Romans and Vandals had each in turn ruled over the Mediterranean Sea without suspecting the secret of this lost land on a deserted coast. The Franks, Crusaders, Moors and soldiers of the Revolution had moved in and one after another pillaged it without guessing a thing... And now it was Aristide Cordat, Doctor of Medicine from the University of Paris who had happened upon this 2000- or 3000-year old inheritance completely by chance—and maybe with another treasure of physiological secrets—to use one or both for the good of modern civilization, if he could only figure out how to take it away safely!

What to do? Before anything he had to figure out where he was and keep his discovery safe. He had to leave the Phoenician crypt and then come back to get his hands on this invaluable store of riches that had probably been ignored even by those who had guarded it from time to time. But first he had to get out! To get out of that bloody jail where they had started to dissect him alive and would no doubt have ended up dissecting him dead. With his gun! He would go out shooting if he had to, or throw gold ingots and diamonds and rubies if it would help him escape this prison of murderers! And too bad for whoever got in his way if he came back in force!

With this idea on his mind Aristide continued his voyage of exploration. He went back again through all the cultivation galleries that he had been through before and was suddenly struck by the fact that the irrigation of the crops surely led to a common canal and the canal must have flowed into the sea. He followed this clue.

This time he was on the right track! Under the ramp that had led him to the upper floor, he found another ramp that led down and turned into a bank of an underground river formed by the irrigation channels. He followed the river along the stone sidewalk and saw that it lead to a 30 or 40 foot waterfall, dropping into a wooden turbine that it moved horizontally. Around the turbine were the generators that it drove and that fed the electric lights by a cable going to the upper floor. A little farther on the waterfall continued its course down a stairway formed by large slabs and it finally flowed onto a bed of sand under a rocky vault that formed a grotto just like where the doctor had pushed his boat.

Two voices! He stopped to listen. The voices were speaking Italian.

"We can't do anything about the propeller! It's only bent, but you need a forge to straighten it out. Let's just do what we can."

And then he heard the sound of saws, hammers and nails over a Neopolitan song, "Marinarella," that the workers sang at the top of their voice.

Aristide was sure that he was a few feet away from his boat, which was sheltered a little farther from the entrance to the cave. He hurried up, turned a corner of rock and...there it was! He was right. Baselli and his two partners were busy repairing the yacht.

All of a sudden he sprung out of the shadows and said, "Hey, friends, how's the work going? Have you made some progress?"

Baselli and the two others were very glad to see him and gave him a great welcome, thinking he had come up, of course, while they were hammering. Right away the good fisherman told his story.

"Ah, *signore, caro signore*! How delighted I am to see you! I was terribly worried about you when I didn't find you at the house and even more worried when my daughter told me about your trip. That damned Nurri plain has such a bad reputation! We waited for a day, but couldn't make up our minds what to do. Then I told myself that, all things considered, our first duty was to look for the boat where you said it was and follow your instructions. You gave me the money and put me in charge of bringing a couple of good workers here to make the necessary repairs; you said that the boat was in calm water at the entrance to the grotto in this bay. First of all we had to get to work! If you came back, everything would be okay. If not, we would go to Cagliari to ask what we should do. So, we started bringing the boards over to the bay. Then we came down and looked for the boat, which we found in no time. The repairs are not serious, at least those that we can do. My partners and I got to work and now it's done. We finished the basic repairs in two days.

With the tar and tow on deck we can do the calking. Your boat will then be ready to take to sea and if you go to Cagliari or somewhere else, they can straighten out your propeller for you, which is not a big thing but better if done by mechanics at a port with the means that we don't have here. Have we done okay?"

"The best you possibly could, my dear Baselli, and I can't thank you enough because I wouldn't have done any differently. In fact, there was nothing else to do."

With that said, Baselli introduced his partners to the doctor as the best carpenters in Gonargientu. Aristide shook their hands and after checking out the work thanked them very much, which clearly made them feel good. The work was almost finished.

"Another two or three hours after lunch and we'll be done, at least with the carpentry! After that it'll only take a few hours to do the calking and painting. But we're waiting for Pia. She's supposed to bring us food. I hope nothing has happened to her. I always come before she does."

"Let's go look for her together," Aristide offered.

The two men had barely left the grotto when they saw the young woman coming toward them at the end of the beach. She was carrying a heavy basket on her head with the grace and strength of a Kanephora, those ancient Greek basket-bearers. She was so happy to see the doctor that she almost dropped her bundle. But she pulled herself together when the two men caught up with her.

"Ah, *signor dottore*," she said, "I'm so glad to see you again! I was dying for four days after you left us. I wanted to go look for you, but my father wouldn't let me. 'Signor Dottore doesn't need us!' he said. 'He knows more than us poor fisherman and will know where to find us when he wants to. Our only duty is to follow his orders.' Thank God he was right and you've come back! But what happened to you?" she spurted out when she saw his left arm wrapped up. "Are you hurt?"

"It's nothing, a simple hunting accident that will be better in no time at all. My gun went off went I was going through some bushes," he added to ease their minds. "I holed up with some good folks who took great care of me. And since I had already been enough trouble by asking them to get medicine for me, I figured there was no use bothering to send them to you, even though I was not sure that you would be here when I came back."

"And except for your accident, do you have any news?" the young woman asked, unable to resist the desire to know about what was so dear to her.

"Nothing yet, Pia: I was laid up by this setback. But maybe I will be luckier in my search now that I can start it up again."

And chatting like that they came to the grotto. The workers were happy to see their food arrive and gave a grand welcome to the young woman who unpacked the provisions on a flat rock: a wonderful *lonzo*,[4] a huge polenta, fruit and two bottles of wine. She took out a tablecloth and set the improvised table. Aristide and the others sat as best they could around the rock and did honor to the menu.

"Tell me, what did you think happened to me when I didn't come back?" the doctor asked while eating.

"By God, to tell the truth, I didn't think any good. This cursed Nurri valley that you wanted to go see is so dangerous and deadly! You see you can't set foot in it without getting hurt! But I knew you were armed and

---

[4] Smoked pork loin.

nothing was making you hurry and you would come back after a little trip in the country."

"And you, Pia?"

"Me? I feared the worst!" the girl said. "But I made up my mind that if anything happened, I would avenge you!"

"Avenge me? How, my friend?"

"Anyway I could! I promised to wait until noon tomorrow and if you didn't come back I would go myself into the Nurri valley and stab the first living being I came across!" she said seriously and savagely.

"Really? You must be joking! How would you do it?"

"With this stiletto," she took out a strong, short blade, sharp as a razor, from her corset.

"And the first living being you came across! That would do you a lot of good."

"That would avenge me. It's very simple. After my brother Orso, seeing someone disappear who went to look for him out of pure kindness, it would have been too much. And I would have done it quick and easy!"

This idea seemed so fair and simple to the listeners that no one said anything against her. As for the doctor, he naturally told himself that it was good that he reappeared because the sudden entrance of Pia into the business of the Tower would have made it hard to arrange the delicate matters that he had to. To change the subject he asked if there were any boards brought from Gonargientu that could be used to build a crate about one and a half or two feet long and six to eight inches high and wide. The workers explained that they had used almost all the wood available, but they had seen that there were some empty crates in the hold that could be used.

Aristide decided to go down into the hold because he did not know where or how to hide the contents of his pockets safely. So, after checking their information he took the opportunity to bring up on deck all the available boxes that had bottles of Champagne and his provisions.

And so he got in a good mood by putting the weighty riches in his cabin and then he gave instructions to build the crates that he needed and said he would sleep on board that night to be ready and able to leave as soon as the calking allowed him to. While waiting, he would devote the rest of the day to a rough survey of the land.

As naturally as possible Pia asked if he wanted a nice roasted goat with some bruccio for dinner. He said he would be delighted, but where would she find the ingredients. She said she would deal with it, so he gave her a gold coin that he got from his leather belt and went walking along the beach to climb the rocks on the right farther down. While exploring the countryside in a direction that he had not yet gone, he thought carefully about what he should do.

He had no doubt that the treasure discovered in the upper gallery of the Phoenician Tower had no owner. Even the nature of the treasure and its abandonment in a kind of dusty attic, open to all comers, covered by the filth of centuries, left barely any doubt that it was *res nullius*, i.e. nobody's property, and anyway was of absolutely no value or completely unknown to the current occupants of the Tower. On the other hand, the occupants amounted only to a new order of harvester ants that he had seen at work, as well as the strange anatomist who had tried to dissect him alive so cheerfully. These owners did not have any interest in the bricks of fine gold or huge precious stones that were hidden in their abode.

Whoever found them in their ancient, artificial covering, had the right to keep them, as if they were found on some desert island or buried in some forgotten tomb. The danger of death that he had faced had, properly speaking, determined and legitimized his findings and gave him the inalienable right to take them *manu militari*, by any means necessary, to use them for the good of humanity. What title of property could be more sacred? He had not wanted or been greedy for or searched for this treasure, whose existence he did not even know about. He had found it, properly speaking, condemned to be discovered through the wildest and most unexpected attack, a blatant attack on his freedom and his life during a devastating trip! And now that luck, or better to say the danger of death, has brought him into possession of this huge wealth that belongs to no one and that no one knows about, would he hesitate to seize it for the good of civilization? No. That would be too stupid and idiotic, not to say criminal! He did not have the right! His strict, practical, hard and fast duty was to get his hands on this boundless latent power for progress. No sensible man in his place would hesitate to fulfill his duty.

That's what Aristide told himself and repeated aloud while striding across the plain and the hills that overlooked the bay.

Suddenly he stopped short on the path he was following absentmindedly. A man and a woman were coming toward him, heading toward the rocky beach that he had left hours before without noticing how much time had passed.

The man was carrying on his shoulders half a goat, skinned, trimmed and ready for cooking. The woman was Pia, all dressed up, balancing a huge bruccio tart covered with green leaves on her head.

And right away she said, "Well, *signor dottore*, have you found any clues about my brother? I'm afraid probably not because you're going the opposite way from the Nurri valley. Too bad! It'll be six soon. Don't take too long, *signor dottore*, if you want to be in time for dinner!"

She went by, straight and slender under her burden, with her consort. And the young doctor suddenly remembered what he had seen in the dissecting room of the Tower. He was struck by the fleeting resemblance between the disemboweled subject next to him on the torture table and the young woman who had just spoken to him.

"Could it be possible that it was Pia's brother?" he asked himself. "The brother whom she cried over and was looking for with an inconsolable heart?"

And the more he thought about it, the more he was convinced. The anatomical subjects could not have been ordinary things on that deserted land that spread out from the Tower. Orso Baselli was taken there, he was sure of it, while looking for the lost goat. He had not been seen again. He had obviously fallen into the trap of that abominable anatomist! It was Pia's innocent brother who was next to him in that cave of torture, a victim of the same crime! It was poor Orso's entrails that he had seen thrown under the table in the sterile bath! And didn't he want to avenge him and himself for the attack? Of course, but first he had to find the assassin and kill him...then get hold of his remains, if only to break the news to the father and sister about the poor young man who was sacrificed in cold blood.

That's what Aristide told himself as he marched over the top of a hill overshadowed by the neighboring summits. The sun was setting slowly behind one of these summits and the shadows warned him that the hour to go back to the bay was coming. He turned around and went back down the path to the sea.

When he saw it again after an hour's walk, a column of smoke was rising from an open fire in the hollow of a rock near the grotto. He sped up and soon saw Pia again. She cried out, "Come on, *signor dottore*, everything's ready. We're just waiting for you!"

The table was set on a big, flat rock at the foot of the cliff. The goat had been browned and cooked medium-well in the country oven and served on dishes from the boat. The guests could serve themselves. One by one they came out of the grotto and sat around the rock. The repairs were finished; the last board was in place and the last nail hammered. First thing in the morning the calking would be done quickly. The crates were lined up in the lower deck of La Mouette. Starting tomorrow afternoon the yacht could leave its bay of refuge and sail to wherever it pleased the captain to go. Aristide was sincerely grateful to the strong workers who had performed this miracle and he toasted them at dinner.

He himself had worked up an appetite on his hike and prepared to attack the roast heartily. He only had one regret: not to have bread to spice up the local flavor. But with a bright laugh, Pia lifted up a white towel that she had spread on the rock and revealed her "surprise"—a fresh, fat, round loaf of bread brought over from the next village with the bruccio tart. While they were cooking she went to make herself up. The wine had been put in the water in the grotto and had time to cool down, but the bottle Aristide had brought up from the hold did not need this extra help.

Each of them got down to their steaming slices of *cabretto* that the doctor had swiftly cut up and passed around. It was so good that after a few minutes there was nothing left of the goat but the bones and a memory. The bruccio tart and the fruits were likewise a hit. The glasses of wine were drunk with equal pleasure and their good spirits were let loose. Finally Pia served the coffee that she had found in the pantry and prepared without saying a word.

The good cheer of the feast was at its height and the evening shadows were already stretching out from the rock toward the beach when Pia suddenly screamed and pointed at an uninvited guest who popped up out of nowhere, coming out of the grotto, outlined in gold by the last rays of the setting sun. It was an individual of medium size, dressed in white cotton and wearing a kind of hood. He hesitated coming toward the group.

At first sight Aristide recognized the anatomist and instinctively grabbed his shotgun that was lying near him against the rock. Next to him Pia got up and went quickly up to the intruder like she was going to ask him what he wanted. He did not say a word. He raised his arm at the young woman who was running up to him and immediately a jet of light mist shot out and surrounded her, like a cloud…

Her legs gave way and she fell gently on the sand. Right away the stranger turned toward the diners and took two or three steps in their direction, obviously meaning to bring down the four men all at once in the same quick way. He did not have time.

Aristide Cordat was on his feet, his gun ready, and with two shots aimed at the head he struck down the enemy who dropped down six feet away from his victim.

For a minute Baselli and his workers were stunned by the rapid crisis, but they quickly got hold of themselves. They ran to the young woman, lifted her up and tried to revive her by patting her hands and fanning her with towels. But she did not move; it was as if she were asleep.

"Don't worry, her pulse is normal and she'll come out of it in no time!" Aristide said after he had joined them. "Carry her back to your house, put her on the sofa and let her wake up in peace. It'll be nothing, I swear!"

"*Signor dottore*, wouldn't it be better to keep her here in the fresh air on the beach?" Baselli suggested, relieved to see his daughter breathing softly like a sleeping baby.

"You're right. Let's leave her in the gentle breeze and just go get some pillows to make her more comfortable."

While Baselli and his helpers rushed to carry out the orders, the doctor leaned over the stranger. He rudely tore the sleeve to uncover his arm. He found a kind of huge antenna in three sections. The first, which was used as a hand, was already beating hard because of a high fever, while the second revealed a glass tube half-filled with a greenish liquid that was fixed up to spray by the contraction of the muscle.

Aristide Cordat pulled off this formidable weapon and he put it in his pocket. Then he lifted the cotton hood that masked the wounded and sat there dazed. Instead of a face that was maybe monstrous but human that he expected to see under the veil, he saw the grotesque, deformed features of a gigantic insect head with strong mandibles and topped by an oversized skull that must have taken the full brunt of the shot because it was riddled with holes like a sieve. It had two facetted, horizontal eyes and a huge frontal eye with three pupils under a bulging blood vessel and puffy tissue. It was the most surprising and the most disgusting face of a giant ant that you could possible imagine.

Aristide glimpsed all this in a second and quickly pulled the hood back down because he heard his hosts coming back with their pillows. He figured it would be better to be the only one to know the secret, so he lifted the wounded, unconscious creature onto his shoulders and carried it into his cabin where he put it on the bunk and closed the door.

Then he went back to the three workers who were fixing Pia up on the pillows as he had instructed. They were preoccupied with their medical orders and barely noticed what the doctor had just done, except to say that he had taken the victim away, which seemed totally natural to them. While helping to move the young woman, he assured them that she was sleeping and had no fever. He ordered them to leave her there for two or three hours wrapped up in a thick blanket and then carry her into the grotto to escape the cold night air.

Then he left them to watch over her and went to smoke on the beach, thinking about what he should do with his wounded prisoner.

4. Negotiations

After long, hard thought, Aristide decided to keep his prisoner alive, since he would have him in his power from then on. He even decided to speed up the recovery since he had the means.

So, he went back to his three companions who were dozing off in the fresh night around the improvised couch of Pia. He told them that she had been exposed long enough to the vivifying fresh air and it would be best now to put her under shelter in the grotto while they waited for her to wake up, which should be no more than a couple of hours. And he immediately started to help them move the sleeper, putting her on the pillow mattress under a well-chosen rock. When she was comfortably set up on the couch he said there was nothing more to do now but imitate her. The three men unanimously agreed to stay by her side and they stretched out on the sand. As for him, he left them and went back to his cabin, lit a big lantern and saw to his prisoner.

He found him where he had left him on the lower bunk of his cabin but not in the same condition. The fever had risen (the temperature was now over 106 degrees) and the pulse was beating fast in his arteries. He was tossing and turning in a silent nightmare that was not transmitted to the palm of his claw by any detectable mental communication, but that Doctor Cordat nevertheless felt was the effect of a dangerous cerebral agitation. In such a case it was completely normal since the patient had received a load of buckshot in his brain.

Being first and foremost a doctor, Aristide told himself that his primary duty was to give all possible care to the sick thing. He soaked his handkerchief in water, made a compress sprinkled with ammonia and put it on the patient's head. After he cut the white cotton that covered him from head to foot he took it off and could then see that the enemy was indeed a gigantic insect—probably a giant ant—with a huge chest above an abdomen that was just as huge, two huge antennae that were used as arms and two jointed legs.

The antennae and secondary legs, six in all, looked atrophied, but were still in a rudimentary state. A black shell covered the body and limbs, as well as the head, like crab's armor. But in spite of the drastic modifications that an extraordinary heredity or maybe a refined art had given to the frightful insect, its general form was still there and left no possible doubt as to its nature: it was a monstrous ant, of the genus *atta barbara*, as tall as an average man and reduced to the four usual limbs of a mammal. But it was still an ant, a reasoning, evil and even learned ant, with a head as big as its abdomen and endowed with strong mandibles, two facetted eyes and a frontal eye with three triangular ocelli that looked like they had been particularly damaged by the gunshot they had just suffered.

As prepared as Aristide was for some kind of full discovery like this, he was just as stunned as at first sight. He took a magnifying glass from his desk and began tirelessly examining and checking all the details of such an abnormal organism.

And suddenly forgetting his personal woes and thinking only of his interest in science, he told himself that he had to preserve such an extraordinary phenomenon in order to get all the information from it that he could. So, the best way to obtain such results might be to resort to the strange medicine whose power he had personally experienced and that was still in its special flask, easy to recognize among the others on the third shelf of the cabinet of dissecting tools. Yes, that was the first thing to do! To go back into the crypt of the Phoenician Tower, find the anatomy lab again and get the flask!

He looked at the wall clock and saw that it was 11:30 p.m. He was sure that everyone was asleep around the yacht. He would never again have such a good opportunity for his project.

He quickly grabbed his lantern, carefully closed the cabin door and went back down into the grotto. Without a sound he made sure that the three workers were sleeping in the sand around Pia, who had not moved an inch on her frilly bed.

He headed toward the fold of rock that hid the entrance to the gigantic stairway. He found it with no problem and marched up. As he was going up he wondered if everything was real, if he was not dreaming, if had really experienced such unheard-of adventures in only a few hours… But of course! There was the riverbed, the sporadic flow where he had come out into the underground foundation of the prehistoric fortress. And there was the stream that fed the turbine and the waterfall rushing down from the higher level after watering the wheat fields in the crypt. There were the final steps and then the crypt itself with its electric lights stretching as far as the eye could see down the hallway. There was the ramp leading to the treasure. There was the endless procession of worker ants carrying their booty to the reserve silos or to the hungry larvae. It was not a dream, but tangible reality! The brave workers were never idle; they were always at work and were not even distracted by the intruder with his lantern.

And finally there was the door to the laboratory! He recognized it, pushed it open and entered the cave where he had been the subject of such horrifying experiments. Nothing had changed. His place was empty on the marble table; the slab was awaiting his return, ready to support his condemned head. A few feet away the disemboweled neighbor still had his chest and belly gaping open; under the table his guts were calmly bathing in alcohol.

Preoccupied with the idea that had haunted him during the day, Aristide brought the lantern close to the dead man's head to see it better: its resemblance to Pia was obvious. There was no doubt: it really was her unfortunate brother who had fallen into the hands of the giant ant to be used as its subject. And how very close he had come to suffering the same fate himself! But it was all over with now, as far as he was concerned. Now it was a matter of dealing well with this adventure that had started so badly, but that from now on would be so simple and promised such brilliant results. To work! To work! Hats off to him who had died in the name of science without knowing it! And especially that his unhappy sister never know about it...

Aristide turned to the cabinet and at first sight recognized the flask that had been used to dress his wound. The faint odor that he smelled was a sure sign. He could still smell it under the bandages wrapped around his dissected arm.

He grabbed the flask and a few other things that looked like a good catch, bandages, compresses, leather straps, cotton shirts and caps; it only took a few minutes.

He soon closed up the tragic door, strode down the hallway of ants and climbed up the ramp to the attic to put some gold ingots and precious gems into a towel that he tied up. Finally he went back down the gigantic stairway and was soon back on board his yacht.

No one had budged. He went back in the cabin and wasted no time getting to work.

After covering the wounded with a blanket that he secured tightly to the four limbs with the help of a double strap, he soaked a bandage in the blue elixir and bandaged the head. Then he put on a compress moistened with the same liquid and over all of it put a band of cotton. Thus wrapping him up like a mummy, he could finally think about getting some sleep himself.

Where was he going to sleep for the night? There was a second bunk that was usually used to throw his laundry and clothes on just above the wounded. He jumped up on it fully dressed and a few seconds later was sleeping the sleep of the just.

At the first light of day Aristide was woken up by heavy footsteps on the bridge above his head. He jumped down from his box and first checked the condition of the wounded. He had calmed down and his fever seemed to have dropped off. So, the blue elixir worked. That was an important point and the perfect opportunity to replace the bandages on the giant ant's skull. The young surgeon got to work first thing. After that he left the cabin, locked the door behind him and with the key in his pocket he went to see the workers. Just as he had thought they were already in the middle of calking the boards and had only good news to give about the young lady they were in charge of. She was still sleeping calmly, which reassured them.

Aristide went to check up on things and found everything as they described. He jumped in the water to wash himself under the rising sun. Then he went back to the workers to ask them about provisions. They thought it would be best to send Baselli to the nearest village to bring back whatever he could get while they finished the calking. It would only take two or three hours. Aristide agreed with them, took some gold from his leather belt and put the good fisherman in charge of bringing back, with whatever help he needed, all the food he could find, especially eggs and dairy products, as well as a couple of bags or a cloth to prepare them.

Baselli left, placing his daughter under the doctor's good care, and promised to be back before noon.

When the doctor saw that the two carpenters were busy at their work and the patients were sleeping well, he decided to go quietly back up into the Tower to bring back a new load of objects—gold bricks, precious stones, medication and grains of wheat. He prepared three of four towels to make the transport easier, grabbed his gun, which he had reloaded, and said that he was going to look around to see if he could find some game. And he gave the two workers a bottle of good wine to be in a good mood for the morning.

After that he left without a sound and pretended to check on the sleeping girl's condition. He took advantage of the workers being inside the yacht to slip into the grotto and find the stairs.

A half hour later he was on his way back with his towels full of the booty he had found and that he had put at the bottom of the stairs to get them when it was convenient. It only took a few trips back and forth between the yacht and the hiding place and soon the various treasures were safe and secure on the boat, some in the crates fixed by the workers, the rest in his cabin where he was eager to get started on a conclusive experiment as soon as possible.

Remembering the effect that a few mouthfuls of ant wheat had had on his own body when he was first in the fields of the Tower, he wanted to try the same treatment on the wounded and also see if it might not help to wake up Pia.

So, he started blowing a few grains of wheat between the mandibles of the monster with a little pipe and happily noticed that by a kind of reflex, or at least an unconscious movement, the mandibles slowly chewed the prey given to them.

It was a kind of unspoken invitation to continue. The doctor hurried to repeat the operation and did not stop until he made the giant ant take in about half a pound of fresh wheat. Then he let the patient digest what he had taken in and went to see the sleeping young lady. He took a flask of ammonia and a glass full of the same wheat that the wounded had just swallowed with such obvious pleasure.

First he put the ammonia under Pia's nose. She sneezed right away, three times, and then opened her eyes. But she was still drowsy and kind of dazed. The doctor then put a few grains of ant wheat between her lips and she started chewing, without looking like she knew what she was doing.

But as the ammonia started working on her brain, she regained consciousness. Soon she showed clear signs that she liked the wheat and was ready for more. Aristide complied. He was glad to see that this time the wheat seemed to go down like candy. After giving her as many grains as he had brought in the glass, he was sure that the truly magical wheat united the most stimulating and vitalizing properties for the nerves with a fast-acting property specific to the muscles. He himself had felt the effects the morning before when he got the strength to make a voyage of discovery through the crypts of the Tower, carry away his findings and go back to the grotto to join the workers repairing his yacht; and all this after suffering several days of total starvation and with an arm still hurting from the most meticulous and cruel dissection.

There was a series of really striking circumstances and the young doctor could not reconcile them to know what to think or expect of them. While he was pondering these things, the sleeper woke up for good, stared at him and suddenly asked, "What have you done with the *bestia*?"

"The beast?" Aristide repeated, taken by surprise and not yet ready with a plausible story.

"Yes, the beast who attacked me with his venom! I didn't have time to see his face, but I saw his hooked feet when I was about to ask him what he wanted. His demon feet, all black, with huge claws. You killed him, I hope, because I can still hear your gunshots ringing in my ears."

"Well, no. I brought him back to health and now I'm basically taking care of him in my cabin."

"You're taking care of him! What are you thinking? Such an evil beast with the devil's claws! You might as well take care of Beelzebub! I'm sure it's him and maybe you can't even kill him. But you can always try. Cut off his head! Does this awful beast talk? Has it said anything to you while you're waiting for it to strangle you to thank you for your care?"

"No, not yet," Aristide was amused by the avenging fury. "I put too much lead in its head, you see, and it's shut him up."

"It must be really wicked to hide its face like a penitent of Saint Francis! You'll show it to me, won't you, when I can get up?"

"Are you strong enough yet?" the doctor asked to call off the dogs before this flood of questions.

"No, not at all, but I will be. My legs still feel numb, like when you're too cold, you know, but they're tingling, which might mean it'll soon be over. So, what did you give me to eat that was so good? I thought maybe it was manna, like the Hebrews had in the desert, as the Holy Book says. It felt like snow on my tongue and it made me feel strong. I'd like some more!" she added like an innocent baby.

"Well, I'll bring you some more in an hour or two," Aristide said. He put his hand over her eyes to stop the interrogation. "You should get some more sleep now and not think about anything."

She was quiet for a minute and when he started to leave she asked curiously, "Where did the beast come from? Obviously from the depths of this grotto since it didn't come in from the front. Do you know if that's where it lives?"

"We'll find out some other time. For now, sleep!" the doctor ordered, slipping away to his yacht. There, too, things had changed.

On the cabin bunk the Beast was sitting up. It had broken the strap around its arms like it was string, torn off the bandage and compress that were covering its face and stared straight ahead with all the facets of its motionless eyes.

Aristide jumped on it and grabbed the two pincers that lay bare on the blanket. Maybe he expected it to put up a fight, but he met with only passive surrender that was literally translated by nerve messages rushing through his fingers. The messages were communicated in the long and short pulses of Morse code.

"Obviously he's going to kill me! And he's right since I would kill him if I were in his place. What a brilliant idea I had to put him aside for vivisection! If it weren't for him I would be free and healthy with four fresh subjects to choose from for my studies. Instead, here I am under his thumb with a broken head and not enough strength even to stand up...not to mention that I don't have my anesthetic pipe. He's going to get even and it serves me right. He isn't stupider than me!"

He stopped for a minute as if he was worn out by the psychic effort, then continued patiently, like he was talking about someone else.

"It's too bad, really! If I know things that he doesn't know, then he, too, might have a lot to teach me about this outside world that I know nothing about, but that would like to know everything!"

Now, without even realizing it Doctor Cordat had already become used to this basic way of understanding his patient's thought as a result of his two experiences; and unconsciously his own thoughts answered the monster, which right away felt them through the palm of its antennae. And these were his thoughts:

"The beast is right! It knows a lot of things that I have no idea about, not to mention the rest of the human species. The two of us could teach each other a great deal, if we could share our knowledge! But how could we do that? We would have to trust each other and make a pact that would put an end to all hostility."

The monster answered immediately, "It's easy. Without my pipe of venom, I'm unable to harm a fly, let alone a man. You've disarmed me. I'll give you my word, if you give me yours. Mine is unconditional and I will trust you…"

"What guarantee do I have?"

"Our mutual interest."

Aristide was quiet. He thought about it.

5. The Departure

"The beast is right," Aristide told himself. "Our hostility makes no sense from the moment that we can understand and communicate with each other. It was obeying its nature and instinct by wanting to dissect me. But all things considered, it was a worthy goal since it was for science. As for me, I shot it in the head and it would have died if I hadn't taken steps in time to get it back on its feet with the proper medical care. We're even now. We both just have to honor the logical pact that comes out of the conflict."

He immediately played the trump that he had been holding back and continued in the mental Morse code, "Since you want so badly to complete your medical studies, why not come and study in one of the great schools on the continent?"

The giant ant seemed to hesitate and think hard about what to say. It finally articulated telepathically, "I am too different from the other students!"

"You mean your physical appearance and your special language?" Aristide shot back. "No doubt you're afraid of being made fun of or harassed and mistreated, which is natural under such conditions. But there's nothing easier to deal with! Concerning your appearance, we could easily give you an artificial human form by using, for example, wax masks for your face, arms and legs, some appropriate clothes to finish it off and…"

"Really? That would be possible?"

"Not only possible, but doable and practical in your particular case. And we could do it so well that you would look almost perfect."

"Oh! I would really like that a lot," the poor monster shouted out, in a way, with his silent tongue, in long and short signals broken by his emotion and surprise.

"Nothing would be easier, believe me, and I'll deal with it right away by sending a telegram to the most qualified specialist in Paris."

"Oh! Do it! Do it, doctor and I will be forever in your debt, which might be paid back by some very valuable information."

"We can talk about that later. Leave it to me to get it done. And to tell you the truth, your language is not very familiar among our learned men, even though it's got its advantages in its way, so you have two choices. In the first place you can use sign language, which is used by the deaf-mute among us and that many doctors and scholars in Europe understand. Secondly you can speak through a portable machine called the phonograph, which you will learn to manipulate easily."

"No! It's not possible! I can't believe it!" the poor ant cried in his mental signals. "You'll do that? You'll manage to give me a human voice?"

"I have no doubt that you can do it if you're ready to make the effort and help me along. But first of all, I have to ask you something."

"Go ahead! I'm all yours and whatever you ask, if you give me speech, I will owe you forever."

"Do you know about the treasure that's hidden in your Tower?"

"What treasure?"

"The stock of gold and precious stones, probably Phoenician."

"Well, no. But it doesn't matter. We have more wheat than we can eat and when I need cotton or chemicals or glass or something, I just sell some wheat at the market in Cagliari through an agent who's been making these transactions for a long time."

"So, you don't claim ownership of this treasure I'm talking about?"

"Not at all and I wouldn't know what to do with it. It's yours if you want it."

"It might be necessary for the project we're planning."

"In that case, it's yours to do with whatever you can."

"I've already brought a few samples here," Aristide continued as he opened one of the drawers full of clay bricks and balls to show to his patient.

"Ah! You found those in the old attic at the top of the ramp? If you can get rid of them and make some profit from them, that would be great."

"I'll make millions from them, which will help us renovate science and, in your case, renovate your appearance first of all."

"Very good. Everything is for the best. Do what you want with these old things."

"Do you have any idea where they first came from?"

"Well, no. I don't really care about them very much and never thought about it."

"I tend to think that they were piled up there by an ancient people we call the Phoenicians."

"That's very likely. My grandfather, whom I was very close to, taught me all the traditions of our race and talked a lot about these Phoenicians who probably came here in their ships on their return from some long expeditions."

"Your grandfather didn't know them, did he?"

"Oh, no! He wasn't that old! Like most of the members of our family he barely lived more than 100 years. I mean 100 complete revolutions of the Sun around the Earth because that's how we measure time. He used to say that the Phoenicians dated back to 5000 or 6000 years before our time."

"Your grandfather was very well informed. Is he the one who taught you anatomy?"

"And everything else I know. I lost my father when I was still very young."

"And your mother?"

"I don't have one. You should know that among us the mother dies giving birth and even if it wasn't like that, we couldn't tell them apart. All our children are raised together in common in our nurseries."

"Do you have any children?"

"You mean a successor to the supreme government of our people? Not yet. When the time comes, I'll choose the best larva, the most gifted of the ones the nurses have raised. I'll take the appropriate measures to develop its brain and other organs to the proportions necessary to governing as it will and I'll begin its education…"

"So, your size and your own faculties are the result of a special treatment determined by your role as chief of the race?"

"Of course. Isn't it the same with you?"

"Unfortunately, no! And that's probably why we're so badly governed."

"That's inevitable!" the giant ant replied with conviction. "And it's surprising that with such a bad method you have managed to survive in the world and sometimes even learned something new. Because I don't have to tell you that there are some things you have knowledge of that we don't!"

"You too, judging by some of your accomplishments. For example, I'm very curious to know how you'll manage to increase the size of your son's body and the volume of his brain."

"It's the simplest thing in the world. By feeding it ant wheat and licking it regularly after treating my tongue with a concentrated elixir. As far as the atrophy of the limbs that we want to leave in their original size is concerned, we achieve this by doing the opposite, I mean by tying them up to prevent overnutrition in the place."

"And these elixirs? What are they made of? I can't help admiring the fact that you can repair living tissue almost immediately, grow it beyond normal size as much as you want, strengthen your muscles and other really amazing things."

"We'll talk about that and I will hide nothing from you when you have initiated me in the miracles of your own civilization. For the moment let me just say that the common base of all our elixirs comes from our own body, treated in special ways. For these preparations we use our excess population, which would quickly become too large if we didn't bleed them systematically. And when our extra ants have distilled all the formic acid we need, we consume their remains. We've become used to this important resource."

"You mean to say that you eat your dead? Properly speaking, you're formivores?"

"That's exactly right. Anyway, it seems that in Africa and other places you do the same thing, eating your own kind, according to my grandfather. But for you it's purely a delicacy and not to get the stimulating, fortifying effects from this good habit like we do! Of course, your goal in this case is mainly to get rid of the corpses because if I'm not mistaken, it hasn't been long since you learned, and not very well, the art of embalming?"

"It's because the matter doesn't get the attention it deserves among us anymore," the doctor answered rather embarrassed. "But a more pressing matter is what I can do to make it more comfortable for you here? Is there anything you need?"

"Since you ask, I will answer honestly. I would like to have a little of my purple elixir, which will make me feel better right away. But you'd have to take the trouble to go back to my medicine cabinet."

"Maybe I wouldn't even have to leave the cabin," the doctor replied and he went to look among the bottles that he had brought back. "Here you go, the purple liquid…"

"Perfect! That's just the thing. I see that you have already thought of everything," the wounded creature said. He casually took the flask and dropped a little liquid on one of the compresses, which he immediately put it back on his head. "In a few hours I will be on my feet again."

"With 40 or 50 lead pellets in your brain? That would be amazing!"

"You can count on it! And what are your plans? Do you have to stay here for a long time?"

"Not at all. I would like to leave today or tomorrow. And if you agree, I'll bring you with me. I can send a telegram to Paris from Cagliari with my orders and when we get to Marseille, we'll find the casts we need for your transformation. I'll put them on in this very cabin and we'll take an express train right away. When we get to Paris, we'll find a quiet place to stay and I'll put the finishing touches on your disguise. Then we can decide what to do for you to learn what you want and for us to make good use of your own knowledge. How does that sound to you?"

"Perfect. And I can't thank you enough. I only ask permission to go back to the Tower for a minute to get some things that are indispensible. And I need to give some instructions to the regent."

"We can talk about that when you're on your feet. You understand, of course, that I am serious about everything; I have your word?"

"By the name of Spiridon!"

"That's your name?"

"My family name, according to my grandfather. We don't use it very often, as you can imagine, but it is apparently very old and dates back precisely to those Phoenicians we were just talking about"

"5000 or 6000 years old! Well! Not too many families today can say that. If it's all the same to you, we can keep it between us and give you a name that will throw off the snoopers. We can say, for example, that you're Manchu or Japanese and your name is Baron Tasimoura and that you haven't learned any European languages yet. This would be completely normal and explain all the eccentricities of your behavior."

"That's great!"

"Well, I'll let you get a little rest and I'll go see about your victim."

"The young lady I put to sleep?"

"Exactly. It's vital that she doesn't see you because I think she holds a grudge."

"So what! It wouldn't take much to kill her."

"Don't talk like that. That's typically Spiridon. But you have to learn human feelings and practice forgiveness."

"Is that what you want? So, it'll be a complete transformation because to tell you the truth, forgiveness doesn't have much currency among us. We know only about what's useful. When any being bothers us or offends us, wham! We kill it."

"You have to drop these rough ways if you want to look like a true Parisian. I say look like because many Parisians think like you, at times, but they usually don't brag about it. Okay, see you soon. I'm going because it's time for me to see if our project is working."

Doctor Cordat left his cabin making sure to close the door behind him and he went down to the grotto where he found the three workers calmly sitting around Pia's bed. She was wide-awake and clearly feeling better. Her father was glad to see her doing so well when he came back from his mission, loaded with food.

The two carpenters were finishing their work and declared La Mouette ready to sail. They all agreed to get it back in the water after a good lunch and they wasted no time preparing it because it was already one in the afternoon.

Right after lunch, they got down to work. They soon had the little yacht out in the bay near the sea and they anchored it with a grappling iron. While they were doing this, Aristide went inside his cabin to write a telegram that he was going to ask Baselli to take to Cagliari. It took him quite a long time to get it right because it had to be precise and detailed. It was an order for Ozoud in Paris to send him by return post as soon as possible to the station in Marseille, various wax and leather "clastic" or prosthetic devices that he wished to receive when he got there.

As he was leaving his cabin and closing the door behind him with his telegram in hand, he was surprised to find Pia standing on the deck looking through the frosted glass at what was happening down below. She looked surprised and confused to be caught in the act, red-handed in her devouring curiosity and pretended that she had come to help her father bring the pillows back to the house since she was walking fine now.

"That's amazing, my dear," the doctor said as seriously as possible, "because I was counting on leaving right away and asking your father to bring an urgent telegram to Cagliari for me. His two friends were supposed to help him bring you back to your house and, because you know how to write, to ask if you would be kind enough to send me word that you were doing all right. I was supposed to get it when I arrived in Toulon at the address I gave."

Pia looked a little taken aback, but she did not try to protest her innocence. Her curiosity was utterly piqued by the presence of the Beast on board and also by what she had just discovered in the grotto.

She was barely able to stand, but as soon as the yacht had been put into the water she took advantage of the moment to run to the back of the cave and see with her own eyes that there was a gigantic stairway. Where did it lead and what was upstairs? She did not know, but the Beast must have come from there and she had to find out about its home at all costs, since it was a mystery. But for now, silence! And without telling anybody about her discovery, she rushed to get to the yacht in its new mooring.

However, Doctor Cordat had gone up to Baselli and given him his instructions. He also gave him two 100 franc bills to share with his partners and asked him to make sure his telegram got to Cagliari. The good fisherman thanked him profusely, saying that the money was much more than the work deserved. Aristide told him that he could never give him enough for his faithful service and that as soon as he got to Paris he would send him even more for his daughter's dowry in honor of the risk she ran on his behalf.

The excellent man was moved to tears and could not express his thanks for the unexplainable generosity. The doctor embraced him in friendship, hugged his daughter and begged them to always regard him as a true friend. Then he shook the hands of the two workmen and asked them to get on their way. He said he would fire his gun in a goodbye salute as soon as he saw them at the foot of the hill that looked over the bay and he would wave to them. With that said they started back and soon disappeared on the path.

The doctor went back into his cabin and found Spiridon on his feet, ready to go back into the crypts with him. They got there five minutes later. Aristide filled a bag with bricks and balls. The ant king gave his orders with a lot of tactile messages during a lively meeting with the Regent and went to the end of the gallery to get the little things that he was bent on taking with him. Then they went back down the gigantic stairway and ran to get on board. Just as they got on board they saw the handkerchiefs waving goodbye at the foot of the hill and right after lifting anchor to take to sea he saluted his friends with two gunshots.

It was 3 p.m., the breeze was fresh and everything was going as planned.

6. In Paris

La Mouette had a good crossing. Two days after it had left the east coast of Sardinia, it arrived in Toulon at the same place in the harbor where it had lifted anchor ten days earlier.

Its crew consisted of only two people, Doctor Aristide Cordat and the ship's apprentice whom he had lost at sea. He only had to put Spiridon in bed and say that he had been sick in order to pass him off as the missing sailor; he showed his papers to the same officer who had signed his "leave." To speed things up and avoid any difficulties by skipping a careful inspection, Aristide said offhandedly, just as the officer came on board, that the sick man had died of smallpox and he did not want to send him to the hospital for fear of contaminating the whole camp. With that the worthy administrator did not ask for anything but to leave the yacht as soon as possible. Aristide held him up for a few minutes out of spite, on the pretext of finding out the family's address so he could write to them in a few days to tell them the sad news, pay his respects and send the few little things that the dead man had left behind.

"This evening I'll send you the address," the other said as he slipped away fast to jump onto his whaleboat.

The doctor spent the day getting some extra supplies and tying up some loose ends. The next morning he got the information he was waiting for and took to sea, heading for Marseille. La Mouette arrived after 12 hours of sailing through a splendid night and anchored in the old port in front of La Canebière at the quay reserved for yachts.

Here again Aristide made his passenger get in bed and right after the customs' visit in the morning—a simple formality since he came from Nice with his papers in order and nothing to declare—he took a carriage to the branch of the Bank of France where he very quickly negotiated for a private safe to store his three crates of precious material. At the same time he made sure that the Bank would buy the gold bars from him by weight and in cash and would negotiate the sale of the precious stones that he would entrust to the head teller.

When this business was taken care of, he went to the station where he happily learned that the package from Ozoud had arrived the night before. He called for it and took it away. All this took around two hours, after which he went back to the quay and boarded La Mouette.

Spiridon was very glad to see him return and told him that when he was gone some snoopy people had tried to come on board a few times, asking to look around or to speak with the owner. He put up the sign that had been prepared for such an event: *Entry forbidden temporarily for repairs*. As they had agreed, he stayed hidden and waved a brush dipped in black paint in front of one of the portholes. After that the snoops stayed quiet and went away.

So, Aristide unwrapped the package from Ozoud and found that his instructions had been carried out to the letter. The wax and leather mask, provided with two glass goggles, fit easily onto the ant face of the poor creature. A black wig covered most of his head and the three frontal eyes; the leggings covered his feet; his arms and deformed hands were stuffed into gloves. It was finished off with a pair of heeled ankle boots and appropriate clothes; he put on a sailor's cap and grabbed the bamboo cane—all together it was a makeshift illusion, but good enough.

The doctor promised himself to improve it in Paris with better devices, but was satisfied enough to try it out that evening by taking Spiridon in an open carriage to dine at a popular restaurant on the Corniche.

They entered almost unnoticed because the garden where they took their seats was pretty much deserted. The waiter alone who came up to them looked a little surprised when the doctor ordered only rice pudding and bananas for his guest. But he was used to serving Chinese and Malay guests so he was not too astonished at the strange traveler that the "captain" had with him. And a minute later he forgot all about it.

As for Spiridon, everything he saw interested and amused him a great deal. He did his best to imitate the gestures of his host when putting the grains of rice in his artificial mouth. He was delighted to taste everything and at dessert he was not afraid to go at the cup of coffee, which he also liked, and even some lemon ice cream, which was delicious to him, even though it was a little cold, as he honestly confessed in his tactile language.

After dinner the two friends left and made a tour of some streets with plane trees. Then they went to the Theatre des Variétés and got a box on the first floor.

Spiridon was not very interested in the novelty of the show and not very amused by the acting. He got tired fast because he did not hear a word of what was said on stage. Seeing this Aristide took him to the Loyal Circus where the poor monster had a great time seeing the clowns do all their tricks and the bareback riders jump through their paper hoops. The horses were especially amazing to him, like supernatural beings.

But he got tired again pretty quickly and did not mind leaving to go back to the yacht where he slept like the deaf thing he was, after taking off his legs and gloves like a human takes off his boots.

First thing the next morning Aristide got a bag of peeled bricks ready and some precious stones that he brought to the directors of the Bank of France. For the gold bars the business did not take long. After weighing them and evaluating them they gave him a receipt by opening a checking account that he could change into cash anywhere. As for the stones—diamonds, rubies, emeralds and sapphires of rare beauty—which were highly praised and said to be worth 30,000,000 at first sight—they could only give him a temporary detailed account with descriptions, weights and estimated value. They accepted to offer them for sale on the European markets and put the money in his account on their sale.

When this important business was taken care of, Doctor Cordat went back to the yacht and hired a young sailor, whom his friends called "Bonaparte" because he was from Ajaccio, to guard it. Then he left again with Spiridon in a carriage to take a tour of Marseille.

All day long they walked from La Joliette to Notre Dame de la Garde, and from Chartrons to different parks and museums in the city without his companion's exotic appearance causing anything but a passing curiosity.

Around 5 p.m. he took him back to the quay, listened to Bonaparte's report in total satisfaction and hired him as the permanent guard of the yacht with special orders to get the necessary work done on the propeller. He put the remaining gems and their worthless clay into a suitcase that he took with him to have dinner with Spiridon at the buffet in the station.

Once there he reserved two bunks on the express to Paris and as 8 p.m. was sounding he was sitting with his companion in their assigned cabin.

That is how Doctor Cordat and his masked acolyte, on the bright and sunny morning of August 28, entered Paris with no drums or trumpets, only a leather suitcase in hand.

"Nothing to declare?"
"Absolutely nothing."
"Go on, Messieurs."

In the station courtyard they caught a cab with a taximeter, which was the new fashion, and were taken to Place de l'Etoile, to a furnished house near the Arc de Triomphe, which Aristide had known about for a long time and that was pretty much vacant at the time. He went to the second floor with "Baron Tasimoura from Hong Kong," and paid full rent for himself and his travel companion. They each took a room on either side of the drawing room and with no further ado went to look for a permanent residence.

That same evening he found a magnificent town house with a big garden on Avenue du Bois and gave two famous architects carte blanche to buy whatever they needed to transform the premises as soon as possible. Then he went to Ozoud to order the prosthetic devices in wax, cotton and gutta-percha or natural latex, which he decided on after his first experiment. He had given precise orders to a tailor, boot maker and hat maker for his student's necessary clothes and started to civilize him as best he could with regular lessons in general studies combined with constant visits to all kinds of museums.

Since he was in constant contact with the giant ant, Aristide had quickly learned much new knowledge that was probably the fruit of age-old tradition dating back, no doubt, to the Pharaohs and Phoenicians and that could bring invaluable help to contemporary science. But at the same time, he had become convinced that Spiridon personally was a little hopeless from both the moral and physical point of view. There really was a gulf between the nature of an ant and that of a modern human. Not only were their vital organs and their inherent nature profoundly different, but also their way of thinking and their motives for acting had nothing in common or even analogous. This phenomenon had often been observed between men of different races and upbringings. It gave rise to real gaps of conscience between a European and an Asian, between a White and a Yellow and a Black and a Redskin. But here the break was blown out of proportion. It arose from a fundamental difference in the physiology itself, in the nature of the primary organs and in the timeworn habits of thought.

Spiridon the giant ant remained completely and necessarily an ant. His clothes on the outside could not change his essence on the inside. Always and everywhere he thought and acted like an ant. For example, he was attracted to the positive sciences by a tireless curiosity; he was hungry to dig deep into them and observe the results. But once he found out, he did not care in the least to use the lessons learned for his own species.

Moreover, he did not want to tell his teacher about any of the findings that his ancestors had come across by chance or tradition. It was not that he was particularly devoted to the ant nation and felt the need to keep the secrets to himself, no. His feelings about this were stranger and more complicated—like selfishness on the part of all his people, stubborn carefulness or contempt for everything that was not traditional.

In one of their daily telegraphic interviews he was explaining to Doctor Cordat the habit of his fellow ants to kill in cold blood any living being that came among them without needing to give a valid reason for the custom. Ants in particular were always killed on the spot when they were not with their own kind. Why? He did not know. That's how it was, nothing more. His people did it at first sight without orders and without any known motive. It was not because they were afraid of a food shortage, since they always had more than they knew what to do with. Tradition, that's all. It was the same when they needed to kill 3000 or 4000 of their fellow ants to eat them after extracting a few bottles of formic acid—no moral or emotional consideration will stop them. They kill and eat their brothers and sisters without even thinking about it the day after they have sacrificed or massacred thousands of beings of another race to defend a single ant.

These characteristics were difficult to understand and even more so to explain. They seemed to be the result of a special mentality, completely foreign to the manners, at least on the outside, of kindness and goodwill that had become current in the human species. Spiridon was not familiar with this kind of hypocrisy, even with his teacher. He always said and did what he liked, especially behaving like a kind of curious artist, but really unable to believe he was bound to any rule of propriety, morality or gratitude that was accepted in civilized society.

It was useless for Doctor Cordat to talk much or directly with his student about this, he could not get used to the extraordinary apathy toward all the opinions received and accepted by men. He had also determined to have some fun with it, like some psychic peculiarity to which he alone had the key thanks to an unheard-of adventure and a perfect knowledge of Morse code.

Sometimes, however, he happened to try to steer Spiridon by reason and example toward ideas that conformed better to the average development of humanity. He did not manage very well and ended up one day forcing him to admit that, very sincerely, he thought the ant species was superior to the human species. Aristide wanted to know how and why. Spiridon said that ants, regarding their social conduct, always thought in terms of the species and not in the rather uninteresting terms of the individual, obviously because they had come to a higher degree of social morality, which humans will reach only after many long centuries.

And since the doctor was caught off guard by this remark, he did not know what to say against it. Spiridon added that in his mind one of the fundamental mistakes of contemporary philosophy was to attribute the intellectual and moral superiority of their species to individuals who were "dolichocephalic," that is, with a long, narrow head, whereas the superiority of the "brachycephalic," the round or broad heads, could not be denied among all the mammals, fish and insects. And right away he rattled off a huge number of positive proofs (contrary to the theories of Gobineau, Ammon and Francis Galton), adding that such a serious mistake could call into question the future of humanity—which, moreover, continued to wage stupid wars from one nation to another and from one individual to another: wars that did not even have the excuse of weeding out the bad to improve the species but rather ended up bastardizing it, killing millions, in every generation, of the best and strongest to preserve the weakest, which was exactly the opposite of an intelligent and reasonable method.

Here again Aristide Cordat was forced to tell himself how true Spiridon was in his social point of view as he over abundantly proved the gradual weakening of warring nations over the last three or four centuries.

"Basically," Spiridon said, "to wrap up this argument, in your general customs you are acting against the teachings of your own science and you couldn't do otherwise if your goal was to ruin and bastardize your species rather than improve it and make it really worthy of the supremacy it pretends to have. As for me," he added boldly, "I see only one trace of civilization and progress in your social habits—alcoholism, which is more and more common and which at least has the benefit of speeding up the disappearance of the weak and useless! Regarding this the only responsible and perceptive lawmaker of your race was Lycurgus, who pitilessly put to death the people whom you let decimate your species with their vice."

Aristide did not have much to argue about with these theories. He dismissed them, telling his student to worry less about his race and more about himself and to do his best to fill in the obvious gaps in his education. For example, he managed to get Spiridon to admit the usefulness of writing and he made swift progress, as well as in the most common languages, especially French and English because they would give him access to books that were not yet translated into Italian.

On the other hand, he showed little interest in sign language, which would have allowed him to communicate directly with many learned men, or for the phonograph, which would have done the same thing in a different way. All this was of little value because he saw in it only one opportunity to reveal the discoveries of his people, which he became more and more stingy with.

As for music, painting and sculpture—they were of no interest to him and not worth his time or attention any more than the architectural monuments or municipal governments, which his teacher tried to interest him in.

The great mechanical industries, the railroads and the river and ocean transports piqued his curiosity more. But he could not understand why men did not concentrate more effort on the intensive cultivation of food products, in which they still used primitive processes—subject to bad weather and risking hunger through their negligence and carelessness.

On the other hand, he had infinite respect for physics and chemistry. He could not understand why Europe, with all the vast and varied resources at its disposal, did not take better advantage of them to develop truly remarkable medicines and especially agents for energy and rehabilitation with well chosen and well controlled foods that were needed—instead of always searching tirelessly for devastating explosives, useless tinctures and deadly poisons.

In his ambition to prove his know-how Spiridon decided to complete the little collection of chemical products brought from the Phoenician Tower by making them himself. But he took the strictest precautions to guard the secret and pitilessly disappointed Doctor Cordat in this respect. But the doctor did not give up all hope. He was counting on chance, his closeness and some offhand remarks to gradually get the essential information about what interested him. So, as far as he could he supported the mystery that Spiridon surrounded himself with and even suggested to him to shut himself up in his laboratory and go in person to the different stores to get what he needed for his preparations—always written out beforehand on prescription forms.

Two or three months flew by like this while the work was being done on Avenue du Bois de Boulogne and the move was being prepared. Aristide had written to Baselli and thanked him effusively for his faithful help and sent along the small sum destined for Pia's dowry. In Marseille he was in direct contact with the boatman Bonaparte who had overseen the repairs to La Mouette. From the Bank he slowly received the very important profit from the sales of precious stones that he had entrusted it with and that it was putting up on the appropriate European and American markets. These regular installments always came on time to pay for the construction bills to transform and decorate the new home. Little by little the walls were raised; the gardens and greenhouses were replanted by skilled workers; the art was bought and set up. In a word, everything was done at the same time up to the day of the sensational housewarming party that would get Paris talking.

While waiting, Aristide carefully avoided doing anything that might give himself away. He lived simply and quietly, kept the habits of his studious youth visiting hospitals in the morning and devoting his afternoons to his personal work. Then when the time came to sound the drums he himself invited his teachers and favorite peers to the party he was throwing.

So, the princely celebration and the sensational operations performed there burst upon Paris like thunder. The comparison is not too strong since it also describes the socialite gossip and academic discussions that were fed for several weeks.

The witnesses invited to the electrifying surgery insisted on giving the details. They unanimously vouched for the extraordinary anesthesia, the simplicity of the operation and the regeneration of tissue that was seen at first an hour later and then over the following days.

The facts in and of themselves were undeniable. How could they be explained and what strange products had been used to get them? That was another matter. The newspapers soon got hold of the story through two technical journalists who had been allowed to observe. Within 24 hours the name of Aristide Cordat went from obscurity to world fame because papers of all shapes and sizes told what they knew of the event. They published a picture of the young surgeon and gave what biographical details they had about him. The lure of mystery was added to that of novelty because no one could say where the wonder of the day had got the huge fortune that was shown in his splendid set-up and no one could give any explanation as to how he had performed his extraordinary operations. The information gathered about the "Tungus" assistant of these miracles, the Baron Tasimoura, about his muteness, his goggles, his weird face and stiff limbs also played their role in the infernal hullabaloo that was raised.

The medical press joined in to demand, in a way, that Doctor Aristide Cordat explain his operating methods. A renowned member of the Academy of Medicine, Professor Bordier, who had not been invited to the gala for the very natural reason that in a past examination he had, for no good reason, unfairly given a bad grade to the young Aristide Cordat who had made the unforgiveable mistake of not studying under him—Professor Bordier took the floor and as if it were an operation by a notorious rival he basically charged him with using "new methods" that they make a lot of noise about but explain nothing. He stigmatized them as being purely bogus and against the moral code imposed on all surgeons worthy of the name who would "put nothing forward without being ready to prove it and without making public all the details of their actions and deeds."

The eyewitnesses of the operations on Avenue du Bois felt attacked and right away countered that they had not apprised the Academy of the circumstances alluded to because the author alone of the operations in question had the right to apprise the learned body of them where and when he judged proper. But, since it was prematurely brought up within the walls beyond all justice and propriety and since they had been favored with a special invitation to see these surgeries and verify the results, they had to vouch publicly for the methods that were so frivolously attacked…

"We saw them with our own eyes," Professor Merius continued, "and not one of my eminent colleagues who were invited to the event will disagree with me— we saw a huge aortic aneurysm, a double paralysis of the optic nerve and two lungs affected with acute tuberculosis, one after another operated on in less than 20 minutes before our very eyes. And we saw the three patients heartily eating their meals an hour after the session. And we were able to verify by repeated examinations that after two days the lesions, which were observed and operated on, were gone for good. We cannot say more because it is not for us to infringe on the personal rights of the operator of these memorable experiments. Anyway, we will be glad to do it all over if one of our colleagues ever invited us to be witnesses again."

With that the Assembly continued with the agenda and Professor Bordier left the hall in a fit of indescribable rage.

He was not the only one to feel this jealous anger. Among the known witnesses of the operations there was at least one who took no comfort in them: Doctor Joel Le Berquin, the prosector at the Ecole Pratique.

Using and abusing his privileged position as a friend of the hero of the day and being personally authorized to follow up on the progress of the treatment, not an afternoon went by that he did not show up at the house on Avenue du Bois on the pretext of examining the patients. In reality it was not them that he was studying hard, it was the so-called Baron Tasimoura.

He watched his slightest movements and attitudes and tried to bond with him, but always ran up against the insurmountable obstacle of the Tungus' muteness and also, no doubt, Aristide's strict advice against his attempts. Sometimes he easily recognized the artificial aspect of the face of the monster he relentlessly studied. He suspected his limbs were no less fake and he told himself that an anatomical examination of these physical peculiarities could maybe lead him to discover those important methods used by his discrete school chum to become the hero of Paris and the whole world in just a few days.

While waiting for the right moment to submit the Baron to this examination, he began by submitting him to a constant surveillance when he went out, which was almost every day. A former undercover detective, Etienne Camparol, who had been dismissed for some minor professional transgression and whom Joel Le Berquin had happened to treat during a serious illness, helped him in this matter. He began by watching him constantly. He saw that he usually went out in the afternoon and took a cab to l'Etoile, giving the driver a paper written out beforehand telling where he had to go. Repeated stalking showed that the destination was either a distant pharmacy or a shop for chemical products and glassworks.

After some trial and error, Camparol figured out that there were only four or five shops he went to, mostly located in the Latin Quarter and nearby in Les Halles. In his usual way, always pretty simple, he got in direct contact with the salesmen and questioned them over a drink at a local bar. He had no trouble seeing that the regular visits of the Tungus and his mysterious appearance had quickly made all of them curious. In brief, even though Camparol did not get a lot out of all of them, he ended up getting some important information and especially some copies of the prescriptions, which he probably gave to Joel Le Berquin.

He, then, could gather certain facts about the substances used by Aristide Cordat or his assistant to get their results. Of course, this general information did not give the proportions or combinations of the mixtures, but it put the prosector on the right track of certain physical effects and the direction of chemical research that he eagerly pursued, which subsequently made him more, even too curious and fanatical.

As a result of pursuing the goal that little by little took shape in his head—to recreate the procedures of "his friend Cordat" and reveal them to the public as his own findings—he ended up, as usually happens, believing that the means justified the ends and he started going along with Camparol to follow the Baron or he went alone until he could know everything about his habits.

And so one afternoon just as Spiridon was leaving a well-known glassworks shop on Rue Racine near L'Odeon, he suddenly appeared in front of him like he was surprised to meet him in the Latin Quarter and made a sign that he was very glad to see him. Then he took out a notebook and quickly wrote a few words and gave it to his victim.

"Of course you came to visit the Medical School, didn't you? Have you already seen the Ecole Pratique and Dupuytren Museum?"

Spiridon shook his head slightly and the other scribbled again.

"You know what my own specialty is as a prosector? Dissections and autopsies. If you'd like, I can take you with me and show you everything that's worth seeing in our collection. It's just around the corner. Send your cab away so we won't be in a hurry!"

Spiridon was tempted by the offer and paid the cab. He followed his guide to the stairs on Rue Antoine Dubois, turned onto Rue de l'Ecole de Medecine and soon came to the gate of the Ecole Pratique.

The caretaker and a few students who were in the courtyard bowed deeply to the prosector, which raised him higher in the eyes of the giant ant. A minute later Spiridon was brought into the nave of the old Cordeliers Church that formed the main wing of the museum on the left side of the courtyard. He followed him through the galleries with a growing interest. His guide made sure to point out to him with a gesture or a note the rarest pieces of the collection. And the visit took a pretty long time. It was almost 5 p.m. when the giant ant and his guide climbed the narrow staircase of the School of Anthropology to visit the wonderful collection of skulls. It was six when they went back down to the courtyard and headed for the prosector's office.

Night had already fallen and the students had left the dissection wing long before; and Joel Le Berquin could use his personal key to enter the restricted building where he was alone with his guest. And that is exactly what he was counting on.

Just as they entered he turned on the gaslights and locked the door. He was alone with his prospective victim.

Spiridon looked around and saw a cadaver injected with red wax lying on a metal table; another table near the barred window was empty. There was also a blackboard and in a dark corner the vials and pans of a little day lab. Two or three chairs were placed around a furnace. A little tired from his long visit to the museum, he sat in one of the chairs and curiously watched Joel Le Berquin taking a piece of white chalk and writing these words on the slate:

"My dear Baron, you will never have a better opportunity to let me, as a colleague, check the particularities of your anatomy."

He was surprised at this unexpected offer and while he seemed unlikely to give in, he suddenly found his head and shoulders covered with a shroud before he could make the slightest move. His adversary threw him on the ground and held him down under his knees. Almost right away Spiridon realized that the shroud was soaked with a mixture of ether and chloroform. He tried hard to put up a fight, but breathed in the gas against his will and fell backward, already asleep.

The chloroform and ether did a fine job.

When he regained consciousness after who knows how long, it was the black of night. The gaslights were turned off. Not the faintest light penetrated the one barred and frosted window that looked out onto a dark courtyard surrounded by buildings. Spiridon was still dazed by the anesthesia, but understood, like in a dream, that he was held down with cords on a metal table. A vague, cold feeling informed him that he was stripped of both his clothes and his masks. A cold draft from the fireless furnace made him shiver violently and feel even more naked. He tried to move but could not. And for hours on end he felt horribly weak and faint and finally, thanks to a change in temperature, ended up feeling numb and drowsy.

He came out of it toward morning, came back to his senses and took stock of the situation as much as he reasonably could. Clearly he had fallen into an elaborate trap of Joel Le Berquin and was from now on at his mercy, on his ground, with his hands and feet bound to an anatomy table. What could be the purpose of the attack? Obviously it was to torture him, the sure and definitive way to solve the mystery of the physique and origin of his victim. Le Berquin had sensed or guessed that the so-called Tungus did not belong to the human species. Seeing his walk and his counterfeit face, especially his eyes, he had glimpsed the truth and taken the necessary measures to prove it.

These measures were a little hard, of course! But after all, Spiridon himself had never shown scruples in his Phoenician dungeon to get humans to study when they fell into his hands. More than anyone else, he could not be surprised that the Parisian prosector acted just as inconsiderately toward him.

The whole question was to know how far he would take it. Would he go so far as to dissect him? Dead or alive? It seemed like it would be more difficult than in Sardinia. Here you had to think about local habits, always being watched and all kinds of practical difficulties. Nevertheless, he had to admit that Le Berquin was not bothered by scruples and had not balked at an ambush. All this could quickly take a tragic turn.

If only Spiridon could get help from the uniformed caretaker who was in the courtyard when he had crossed the threshold of this cursed School! But, without a larynx as he was, there was no way he could call out—and no one would probably hear him if he could. And as for getting someone's attention by breaking the window or some other violent outburst, it was out of the question since he was tied down to the anatomy table. Wait and see what would happen, that was the logical thing to do.

Spiridon was so convinced by his mental analysis of the situation that he managed to fall asleep again in spite of his worries. Or better said, he surrendered to the fatigue and lethargy that weighed down on him and he fell back into unconsciousness again.

The sound of a key turning in the lock woke him up. Now it was day, a gray, sad winter day. Le Berquin entered, closed the door behind him and came up to the dissection table. After making sure that the captive was still in the same position, he went to the blackboard, erased what he had written before and scratched the following words:

"Well! Have you come out of it? Are you ready to answer my questions?"

Spiridon did not move and gave no sign of life. Le Berquin turned around to face him.

"You could maybe give me some sign if you agree!" he said between gritted teeth. "But I forget that he's deaf as a post and supposed to hear nothing…even though it looks like it's just a bad joke. Let's see what happens if we loosen up a hand to see if he can write."

He went back to the table, untied the strap that was binding his victim's antenna and put pencil and paper in what would be the right hand. Then he went back to the chalkboard.

"Now, are you ready to answer in writing?"

Spiridon did not budge.

"I have to warn you that you are playing a dangerous game!" the prosector continued. "Not only do I have control over your carcass, which is after all only the carcass of an ant, *formica flava*, but I may also have to get rid of you to avoid any problems or complications. It's 9 a.m. I'll give you until noon to think about it while I go make the rounds at the Hôtel-Dieu Hospital. Try to understand that *you have to answer* my questions or else disappear. A word to the wise is enough!"

Joel Le Berquin put the chalk down, pointed emphatically to what he had just written and locked the laboratory door on his way out.

Spiridon did not know what to do. But he had no doubt about what Le Berquin was expecting. Obviously the prosector was planning to extort the secret of the operations that he saw performed on Avenue du Bois de Boulogne. Knowing that he really was a giant ant in the animal kingdom was not enough for him. He wanted the whole secret that Aristide Cordat had not told because he only knew part of it.

Spiridon would not refuse him the secret on principle if it was necessary to save his life, but the real question he had to ask himself was this: If he revealed the formula demanded by his executioner, wouldn't that be a sure way to sign his death sentence? Joel Le Berquin had him in his hands.

To reveal the secret that so many people wanted to know, wouldn't it, in one fell swoop, destroy the only protection that Spiridon had? If he said nothing, it would be in Le Berquin's interest to keep him alive. And if he gave in, he would put himself at the mercy of his captor who would want to make him disappear when he had nothing more to get out of him.

The conclusion of his tragic thoughts was that he had to be clever and trick his torturer into making him believe that he was getting the upper hand, but he would not give in, if there was no other choice, until the last minute.

While waiting, Spiridon remembered that since lunch the day before he had not put a single grain of rice between his mandibles. A voracious hunger started twisting the guts of the giant ant.

"If this brute of a prosector had only thought of bringing me a handful of wheat," he thought *in petto*, "and offering it in exchange for what he wants to know, I do believe that I would not have the strength to refuse him."

And he also told himself that it would be a good excuse for his surrendering that he could not yet leave this world because he had not yet named a successor!

7. An Unexpected Visit

As Baron Tasimoura's absence dragged on, Aristide Cordat felt more and more anxious. What could be the dark purpose of his desertion? Was it by choice or not? That's what he could not figure out very easily. The giant ant's habits were so specific and so mechanical and his days varied so little in their fixed routine that there was not much room for the unexpected. He barely ever left the house except to take a short walk down the broad Avenue or take a cab to go to a glassworks shop or a chemist. Besides, he had no voice and could not talk. His communication with the outside world could only be carried out in writing and it was naturally very minimal. Moreover, Spiridon was set apart from the human race not only by the fundamental difference of his organism, but also by a total lack of sympathy. Outside of medical issues, which he had some knowledge of, nothing about the civilized world really interested him. The prevailing ambitions and passions of the world were worthless in his eyes. So, it was unlikely that he got mixed up in some trivial adventure. The most likely explanation was that some accident befell him, some disaster.

When Aristide did not see him return for dinner, he sent his entire house staff out to get information. The valet came back around eight to say that the baron's usual coach (an Urbaine, number 3207) had left a little before two from the traffic circle at l'Etoile and was not seen again. He was ordered to go back to the cab station and not come back until he found the coachman.

At around ten he brought the man, who had come back to his post. He told him about his odyssey. He was hired at l'Etoile by "the man who gave directions in writing." He drove "following the paper" across Place de la Concorde to the corner of Rue Racine and Rue Monsieur le Prince. There, Baron Tasimoura went into a glassworks shop. When he came out of this shop he met a friend who had obviously made him change his plans because instead of getting back in the cab to go back to l'Etoile as his prewritten note had said, he waved the coachman away after giving him a 100 *sous* coin. The two gentlemen then went down Rue Monsieur le Prince on foot while he himself went back toward Boulevard Saint Germain. That's all he knew.

"This gentleman you saw, who met the baron on the corner of Rue Racine," Aristide asked, "was he young or old?"

"Rather young."

"Around what age?"

"I'd say he could have been in his thirties."

"Wearing medals?"

"No, I don't think so."

"Did he have a beard or was he clean-shaven?"

"Well, I don't really know…I think he had sideburns, but I can't say for sure."

"How was he dressed?"

"Like everyone else. A dark overcoat, I think, and a flat-brimmed hat."

"Flat-brimmed! Are you sure?"

"Well, Doctor, it seemed so, but I wouldn't swear to it."

"You would recognize him again, though?"

"Maybe so, if I saw him…"

Aristide rang the bell right away.

"Jean," he said to the valet, "go get the coach that we have here and take him to see Doctor Le Berquin, whom you know, at 83 Rue Hautefeuille. Ask to talk to him for me. Tell him that I'm very worried about the strange disappearance of Baron Tasimoura who left here today a little before two. Find out if he met him during the day on Rue Racine and if he did, ask him for me where and when he left him. If it's possible, discretely figure out a way to get the coachman to get a look at Doctor Le Berquin to see if he's the one who met the baron on the corner of Rue Racine. This would help me a great deal in my search. And I don't have to tell you to act with the utmost courtesy. If Doctor Le Berquin really is the friend who took the baron with him, as seems likely, and if he can say where and when he left him, invite him to come back in the coach and talk with me. Or at least ask him to set up a meeting with me...as soon as possible. Go and come back right after you find out what you need to. Here's a *louis* to give to the coachman when you're done."

At 11 p.m. the valet was back. He had not met Doctor Le Berquin at his home and after waiting two hours decided to leave a message with the doorman, who promised to give Doctor Cordat's invitation to Doctor Le Berquin when he came back. But it was very likely, he added, that the prosector would not get the invitation until noon the next day. That was when he left his office at the Hôtel-Dieu Hospital. Sometimes he did not show up for two or three days.

The final report was that he should not expect to have any definitive information before the following day. So, Aristide decided to go to bed while waiting for events to unfold.

He slept badly and woke up extremely troubled, especially when he saw that the morning mail brought no letter, telegram or information of any kind about the matter. First thing he went to l'Etoile where he found coachman number 3207 on his seat and he made him repeat the details of the day before. Then he decided to ask the coachman to bring him to the glassworks shop on Rue Racine. There the shop's clerk and cashier confirmed the details given by the automaton. And they showed him the entry in the books that corresponded to Spiridon's purchases, specified thus: glass pipettes following Doctor Cordat's order, two long and two medium, 1,80 francs.

The doctor then went to 83 Rue de la Hautefeuille where the doorman confirmed what he had told Jean the valet the night before. As for the prosector, he was still away.

This fact made the young doctor all jittery. So, he ordered the coachman to take him to police headquarters and he wasted no time giving his card to see the Chief of Police. The dignitary was Captain Brideau, well known to all Parisians as well as the press. He was a short, skinny, blond man with a bristling moustache on the face of a Kalmyk.

After a long wait Aristide was finally taken into the magistrate's office where he told him about his worries about his collaborator and friend Baron Tasimoura and the suspicious circumstances surrounding his disappearance. The Chief of Police had, like all of Paris, heard of the famous operations of Doctor Cordat and his assistant. He took down the name and description of the Baron and the circumstances of his exodus, but did not seem to attach too much importance to an absence that had not yet lasted even 24 hours.

"In Paris these kinds of accidents happen a lot to foreigners," he said, "especially when they are, like your friend, absolutely ignorant of the customs of the country;

and then again, he's mute. You'll see your young prodigy come back in no time after playing hooky and taking a short, spontaneous trip to Versailles or Saint Germain. I wouldn't be surprised if you found him at home right now. Nevertheless, I'll be sure to order an immediate investigation, as you wish, by some of my most faithful agents. The leads you have given me will be followed up on and I'll tell you what we find out. As for you, if you have any news or come across a useful clue, I would appreciate it if you would let me know right away. The telephone is here waiting and my office will always be ready to listen to you."

With that Aristide Cordat took his leave of the Captain and realized as he was going down the stairs that he had completely forgotten to have breakfast. So, he went to a nearby café to carry out the necessary operation and read through the newspapers, secretly hoping to discover some clue about the matter at hand. As soon as he had swallowed his coffee he went back to l'Etoile.

It was almost 3 p.m. when he got back home. As the coach was pulling to a stop, he heard a voice ring out. "*Eccolo, in fine! Padre mio, che cosa abbiamo da fare?*"

Struck by these words and the voice that seemed familiar to his ears, he stuck his head out the door and was sharply surprised to see a young lady dressed *à l'italienne* and a bearded man waiting on the street, sitting next to each other on the edge of the sidewalk on one of those pigskin suitcases that you almost never see except in overseas countries.

The young woman was none other than Pia, escorted by her good father, Signor Baselli. Pia was wearing her formal dress that was a little crumpled from the trip and her hair under a hastily tied scarf was powdered with dust from the South of France. She was carrying two or three bags more or less decorated with petit-point embroidery. As always, in her way, she was beautiful, in spite of the circumstances that were not very friendly to an elegant appearance.

As soon as Aristide recognized her and her good father with their bags, he stopped the cab and jumped onto the sidewalk. Pia ran up to him, grabbed his hand and kissed it hard, carried away by joy and tears. And the good Baselli, although less noisy, was hardly less restrained in expressing his ecstatic joy. The two of them looked like castaways suddenly seeing the rescue boat on the horizon. The passers-by were already stopping to watch the hugs and kisses.

"Why are you waiting for me out here on the street?" Aristide asked. "I guess you've just arrived?"

"Just arrived, *caro dottore*! We've been here for two or maybe three hours waiting for you!" Pia answered with her usual candor.

"You should have waited in my house and freshened up a little!" the doctor said for the stately doorman's information, who had just opened the door at the sound of the bell.

"We couldn't have asked for anything more," Pia confessed, "but we weren't asked, or I should say we refused," she added triumphantly while glancing at the man with the gilt edges who was so snooty before but was now all shamefaced.

"We'll get you to your rooms with your suitcase," Aristide said to cut short any sensitive explanations. "I'm sure you won't be opposed to freshening up a little. When you're done, come down to the dining room. You must be starved!"

A few minutes later the father and daughter had made their brief ablutions and were sitting downstairs at a table set with cold meats and fruits.

"Monsieur asked that you not wait for him. He will join you when he is free," the valet said.

Without needing to be asked twice, Baselli and Pia started lunch. They were obviously impressed by the splendor of the things around them, but they were so hungry that they had no time to waste on empty words. And they did not speak to each other at all during the entire lunch. They were also probably intimidated by the valet who was serving them. A few glasses of old wine had managed to bring them up to the occasion when the doctor was told of the situation and left his office to join them.

"You must excuse me for not keeping you company, but I'd just eaten and had some urgent letters to send out," he said when he sat down with them. "It was a good idea of yours to take the train and bring me news. You were so welcoming to me on my trip to Sardinia that you couldn't have made me happier by coming here!"

"You see, father, I told you so!" Pia said as her eyes sparkled. "He didn't want to come with me to Paris, but I was so set on it that he decided to come so that I wouldn't be alone. We have so much to tell you. You have to know everything!" she continued enthusiastically. "And first I have to tell you that right after you left I discovered and explored the lair of the *Bestia*..."

"What beast?" Aristide asked, knowing full well what she was talking about, but figuring that it was dangerous territory where he did not want to venture.

"The cursed Beast! The evil beast that gutted my brother and wanted to do the same to us!" the young lady shouted passionately in that tone of voice that the islanders of the Mediterranean use whenever they talk, but that here carried a particular weight for the serious events that she was the heroine of. "And speaking of that, where is that wretched beast?" she suddenly glowered at Aristide. "I know it's here and that's really why we came!"

"He's not in Paris. He left all of a sudden without telling me where he was going. I know nothing at all!" the doctor answered, deeply satisfied for the first time in 24 hours that his awkward assistant had disappeared.

"Don't worry, we'll find it, if we have to travel around the world like the Italian emigrants on the train with us from Genoa. There are companies that take you for free!" she explained and waved off the matter. "But back to subject: Yes, I'm dying to be told about what I suspect and that your sudden departure, *signor dottore*, gave me no time to investigate. While I was on the sofa in the grotto I thought long and hard about the attack the day before and about the particularities of the Beast's sudden appearance while we were eating. It obviously came out of the grotto. Was it living there? Or did it come from some deeper hideaway? That's what I wanted to know and what I promised to find out. Taking advantage of the time you were busy with my father and our friends pushing the boat into the water, which left me alone, I ran deeper into the grotto and easily discovered behind a pile of rocks the first steps of the stairway that obviously led to the upper areas of the cliff. That's all it took to put me on the right track. You insisted on leaving right away and to wave to us on the way back to our village before taking to sea. I didn't have the right or the desire to go against your wishes. I accepted and left with the others. But I promised myself to go back as soon as I could and continue to check up carefully on my obsessive suspicions. In particular, did you take the wounded Beast with you? I was sure of it since my father and his friends had carried it to your cabin on your orders. You had your own reasons to take vengeance on it like that. It wasn't for me to challenge your decision, but I thought and still think that I have the right to know the truth about my poor brother's death and about the actions of the Beast who wanted to massacre us. So, I waited for the right time and when my father had to go to the tuna fisheries in Porto Botte to take care of some old business, I took advantage of his absence to go back alone to the bay where you put up your boat...

"Of course I knew the way. It was easy for me to find the grotto again and in the grotto the stairs that I had found. I had brought a bag of food and some candles and along with my stiletto I had an old gun that I took off the mantle and loaded very carefully. Once I was in the grotto I lit one of my little votive candles and started climbing the stairs."

"What can I tell you, *caro dottore*, that you don't already know? Because I think that you, too, found the stairs—before me it seems—and you, too, explored the building. Am I wrong?" she paused.

"That's exactly right," Aristide confessed, knowing that he couldn't deny such a likely circumstance.

"Ah! You see, *padre mio*," the young lady cried out, turning to her father with a triumphant smile. "I was sure of it! And I'm sure that's what we owe our life to! Because when you saw the Beast, you didn't hesitate for a second and you knew what to do about it. You jumped for your gun and shot it twice in a row and that's all it took to save us from the clutches of the vampire! Otherwise we would all have suffered the same fate as our poor Orso."

"What? You know…" Aristide moaned.

"I know! I saw!" the young woman replied in a voice that left no room for doubt. "Less than an hour after climbing the stairs of the old fort and after going through the corridors where that endless procession of ants under their grain paid no attention to my presence—I visited the upper rooms, opened all the doors and ended up in front of that awful sight! My poor brother, gutted and opened like a pig on a torture table—his lungs, heart and all his innards piled up under him in glass jars. Oh! Whoever did that deserves to die! And he will die by my own hand! That's why I have come here with my father, *caro signore dottore*. Don't you think that it's our most sacred duty to avenge such a dark crime?"

Aristide Cordat did not answer the question that was asked of him. He sat there without saying a word, telling himself for the second time that evening that the baron had escaped Pia's revenge just in the nick of time and he definitely had to congratulate his absence, whatever the reason.

"You don't have anything to say? Don't you agree that we need to punish such a foul crime?" Pia asked as she was bothered by his silence.

"Certainly… Of course…in principle!" the doctor muttered. "But we also have to take into account the circumstances that we really don't know very well and also the fact that we are not in Sardinia but in Paris! Here it's customary to let the courts decide such matters," he pleaded. "We can surely take him to court if you'd like."

"Court!" Pia shouted and sneered. "The courts! And who will tell me that they'll see straight? But it's cut and dry! My brother is dead, murdered, cut to pieces…that's what I saw and my father and everyone in the country with us! What do you expect the judges in Paris to do about that? It has nothing to do with them. It has to do with me, Pia Baselli! And I will set things straight without the system, with only my stiletto here…"

She pulled her weapon out of its sheath and shined it in front of his face.

"Hide that, my friend," he said softly. "I assure you that those toys are out of place here. We're not in Sardinia! So, tell me what happened after you visited the *castello*."

"What happened was plain and simple. I don't know if it's the custom in Paris to honor the dead and avenge them when they have been murdered by a cowardly brute with no faith or honor, but in my country, in humble Sardinia, we don't let them disappear without giving them their due. Poor Orso! Dear, good brother who meant no harm to anyone! Who simply committed the crime of following our goat on the lands of a rotten *Bestia*! We didn't want to let him part without giving him the funeral he deserved. Even before my father came back from his trip I had told our friends and the neighboring villages all about it. Hundreds of them came when they found out about my dark discovery. They helped me bury my dear brother. They carried him on their shoulders into our humble abode. They covered his funeral bed with flowers and leaves. And just when my father finally came back and found out the sad truth, all the women from the area were joining my grief and they took turns around the funeral bed all day and night to sing the praises of the dead and the sorrow and sadness of their destiny. Maybe you know that's the custom on our island after a tragic death and the songs are called *voceri*. Then when my father came back everyone from miles around wanted to join in our mourning. Our neighbors came by the hundreds and many people who we'd never even seen before came down from their villages to take their turn and carry the body on their shoulders all the way to the grave where he will rest for eternity. The women and their children were there just like the men. And everyone wept, everyone shared our heartache. We have a heart where I come from, *signore dottore*. Everyone understands that a loved one cannot fall at the hands of a murderer without all honest people feeling wronged themselves. Poor Orso! Dear brother so close to my heart! At least we have honored your remains!"

The poor girl was so deeply shaken up by the memory of the honor rendered to Orso and the people's sympathy with her mourning that she could barely talk; tears streamed down her brown cheeks.

But all of a sudden she continued her story. "If you had seen how all these friends and strangers took to heart the outrage that we suffered! They wanted to show it by their actions and not just by their words. They said, 'It's not enough to honor the one we have lost. We have to prove who we are by completely destroying, getting rid of the last trace of the lair where he was massacred.' And they wanted to tear down the Beast's *castello* stone by stone so that no memory of it would remain on our land."

"Not really!" Aristide cried out, being worried in spite of himself as he thought of the countless riches hidden in the ancient walls.

"Yes, *signore dottore*, that's what they said. But it was easier said than done, as we soon found out when examining up close the *castello's* construction. The stones were huge, real boulders piled up in those incredibly thick walls. Some said that giants must have built them, maybe 1000 years ago, and that no human force could do the job. In short, we gave up the impractical idea until you, *signor*, were so kind as to send that large amount of money…for my dowry, as you said."

8. The Illustrated Newspaper

"To tell you the truth," Pia Baselli continued her story, "we'd never seen so much money—10,000 lira—and when my father and I went to get it at the bank in Cagliari, we just stood there at first, stunned by such a fortune and also by the extreme kindness that made you so generous."

"It was the most natural thing in the world after all the help that you and your father and friends gave me." Aristide said modestly.

"Well, *signore dottore*, do you want me to tell you frankly what we were thinking?" the young lady answered. "We were thinking that you had obviously entered the *castello* before me and discovered my brother's remains and you were afraid to tell us such dreadful news, at first out of sympathy and then, maybe, regretting not to have done it, you wanted to offer us compensation by such a wonderful gift."

The doctor was confused by such a charitable and altogether probable theory of his generosity. He was wondering whether he should not protest, but Pia continued.

"Oh! We didn't want to think such a thing, *signor*! We really did think that so much kindness was truly worthy of you. Anyway, that's how we explained so much goodness that was so far beyond our needs and our wildest dreams. The truth is that we would not have even known how to spend it well if chance hadn't shown us the way. As we were coming back from the bank I noticed the illustrated newspaper *Roma pittoresca* in a bookstore window. And I was very surprised and very happy to see on the front page a picture that looked like you and had your name underneath: *Egregio dottore Aristide cordat di Parigi.* I bought it right away and I got what I'd been wanting for weeks but never dared to ask you for, your picture, our benefactor! I put it in my pocket and we left on the *vetturino* to go back home. My father kept the money the banker had just given him in his waistband and he tied it around his elbow to be sure that no one would steal it from him. And on the way back he suddenly said to me, '*Figliola mia*, this money is weighing on me and I would like to know how to spend it. It you agree, here's what we can do to celebrate and honor the memory of our Orso. You know that my partner and I worked at the naval base in La Maddalena when we came back from Abyssinia. They make a very powerful explosive there that was invented, I think, in England and that they call *cordite* and they use it to destroy smelting works and granite. I think I can pay enough to a friend of mine there, who guards the powder magazine, to get some of this cordite and we can blow up the castle of the Beast. What do you think?'

"I said that it was a great idea and the best way I could think of to spend the bills that were in his pocket! 'Well, I'm going to talk with my partner and if he agrees, we'll try to fix it up.' And that's how it all started. You see, doctor, your money was put to good use! A few days later my father took his precious belt and left with his partner for La Maddalena on their boat, which they had specially sent for from Tunisia. Since they were well known and well respected by everyone as being retired from the fleet and former workers at the naval base, they had no problem getting what they wanted. Besides, I have to say that they acted with the utmost discretion and skill, not only paying the guard what he wanted for the 60 bags of cordite he gave them, but also replacing these bags with a large amount of bills (5000 lira) that they buried in the ground of the powder magazine exactly where the cordite was, in store there for the base's treasurer as soon as there was no danger of establishing a link between their visit to La Maddalena and the deal made with the guard.

"Thanks to their combined efforts the bags were first brought by night to a cove on the coast where the boat landed after taking off from its first mooring, as if to come back home. In this cove the bags were loaded without a hitch and brought very fast to our shore, to the very grotto that you know well…we call it the Doctor's Grotto after you.

"Everything went as smoothly as possible. No one knew or suspected what was being done, so there was nothing left to do but finish off what we were planning. Since they were both old gunners of the fleet and former workers at the base, my father and his partner knew how to handle cordite. They took their time bringing the bags up the underground stairs to the vaulted rooms that could best be used for their plans. From the bags to the beach they used long, sulfured fuses that they laid out from a few well-chosen points of explosion to conveniently protected areas under the cliffs. When they were satisfied with their preparations we went to invite some friends from the area to come that evening and watch the great fireworks dedicated to the memory of Orso.

"The meeting place was exactly where the rock is at the foot of the mountain on the heights that overlook the bay, where we watched you leave. Maybe you remember we waved goodbye with our handkerchiefs? At the appointed time everyone was there, at least 2000 or 3000 people. You can be sure that I didn't miss it. And my father and godfather were at the foot of the cliff in the protected crevasse that they had set up. At 6 p.m. sharp, as agreed, we heard a loud rumble that shook the ground under our feet. A second later there was a firestorm, a real volcano that burst out of the *castello*, hurling all those cursed stones, which our friends thought were impossible to destroy, into the sky among thunder and lightning. They shot up with an incredible force, a couple of miles high, one after another, and fell back down into the sea as far as the eye could see. A riot of burning rocks, blazing and sizzling in the water to the constant cheers of the spectators. Two minutes later it was silent again and instead of the *castello* we saw nothing under the setting sun but a black, gaping hole, a kind of empty crater that took the place of the old fort."

Pia Baselli thought her story was falling on welcome ears, but she was interrupted by a cry of anguish.

"What have you done?" the doctor screamed. "You've destroyed the castle! Oh, you poor, unfortunate people. That's...maybe three billion that you've destroyed and thrown into the sea!"

"Three billion for that dump?" Pia shot back emotionless. "Well, even if it was worth hundreds of billions or millions of billions, it wouldn't do enough honor to the memory of our dear Orso, who was so tragically gutted! But listen, doctor, I haven't told you the rest. At the *vendetta* celebration one of my friends who was there brought me a little frame that I had asked him to buy in Cagliari for your picture. When I got back to the house I took the newspaper to cut out your picture and I saw that on the back of the page not only was there an article about you, but also another picture...of your partner Baron Tasimoura. They said in the article that you had made one of the great discoveries of the century and had performed some supposedly impossible operations in front of your illustrious colleagues. They also said that because of this discovery you were the most famous surgeon of the two worlds, both the Old and the New, and that you had a devoted assistant and partner in your operations, a guy who didn't speak, Baron Tasimoura, a Tungus. I really have no idea what a Tungus is! But when I looked at the picture, I started thinking that your partner was the very same one who you took away from the *castello* and put on your patched up boat after shooting him with your rifle to stop him from hurting us. My father and I first took the stagecoach from Cagliari to Genoa and then the railway to come here to get to the bottom of this. Answer me, *caro dottore*, am I wrong? Are Baron Tasimoura and the *bestia* one and the same being, as I suspect? If it's true, I have to kill it; *it's up to me!* And you won't try to talk me out of it because you are just and you know that it murdered my brother Orso. And that's why I am here. I won't return to Sardinia without fulfilling my mission!"

In face of Pia's ultimatum Doctor Cordat was very embarrassed because he knew better than anyone how right she was and that without the slightest possible doubt Orso's murderer was the apprentice anatomist of the castle—the giant ant. But the anger that raged in him pulled him through, at least in this cruel predicament and faced with such a challenge that was so well founded and so urgent—he unconsciously came up with the right response by talking about nothing but the explosion.

"I don't understand anything that you said about your brother's so-called murderer, who you think might be Baron Tasimoura," he ended up saying, choked up with anger. "Baron Tasimoura could not have done any harm to Orso because he was never in Sardinia and, besides, I repeat, he has disappeared without me knowing why or how. But if there's one thing for sure, it's that your crazy idea of blowing up the castle has caused you an irreparable loss! The fortress that you destroyed and whose ruins now lie at the bottom of the Mediterranean held an incredible Phoenician treasure of gold bricks and precious stones whose approximate value is impossible to guess, but we could easily estimate in the billions. It's all destroyed now, lost, gone up in smoke and drowned in the sea, my poor Pia. Do you understand the incredible harm you have done with your explosion? I'm not just saying to myself, but to Science, which could have benefited from this great treasure and to your father and yourself because you can't deny the happiness it would have brought you."

He uttered this regret now with no bitterness, almost passively, in the pressing need to tell the truth. And suddenly a wild groan burst out in the falling twilight. Pia threw herself face down on the rug, seized by the bitterest, the most unexpected despair. She tore out her hair and scratched at her face.

"*Maladetta ch'io sono! Disgraziata!*"[5] she yelled hoarsely. "I have ruined what I love, me and my father, thinking I was doing good! I threw millions into the sea even though we are beggars! Could I have guessed such a thing? The evil eye of the *bestia* follows me even when it's not here. But I will find the cursed thing if I have to go to his own country, whose name I don't even know and that I'm sure lies at the bottom of hell! I will find it wherever it's hiding and I will cut its throat, tear out its guts and throw them to the dogs to avenge my brother and us and the good doctor who I've ruined. I will do it,

---

[5] Cursed as I am!

I swear, if I have to walk barefoot over broken glass to the ends of the world! And then I will die avenged, maybe even satisfied. Let men heap curses on me, I will not die uselessly in this world of misery and injustice! Cursed, cursed as I am!"

Baselli and Aristide were leaning over her. They lifted her up and calmed her down as best they could, which was not much. Then the doctor got the brilliant idea of making her think of something else, like you do with children, by talking about the cause of her desperation.

"Don't you think," he asked the old sailor, "that the coral fishermen, those divers like they have in the Balearic Islands and in Sicily, could go and search and bring to the surface some of the debris drowned in the explosion?"

"Of course, *signor dottore*!" Baselli answered, clinging strongly onto the idea. "I know where the rubble was thrown and I could take charge of fishing up a good part of it with men like that. If you want, *signor*, I'll hire them myself, with my boat, all along the coast where they live. I'll guide them in their search and let the devil take us if we don't find some of that precious wreckage."

Aristide Cordat knew better than anyone how unreal his hope was. To really think that sponge or coral fishermen would ever find any of the gems or gold bricks that were thrown into the sea or that they would give them up once found, seeing how impossible it would be to claim ownership or hide their value...the idea was obviously crazy; it could lead only to disappointment.

For the moment, however, it did at least have the effect of almost instantaneously calming Pia down by sidetracking her to a new idea.

"That's it!" she cried out, quickly changing her mood, clapping her hands and jumping to her feet. "We'll set up on the seashore, even in the grotto. I'll prepare the food for the fishermen and hear everything they have to say. We'll give them a legal share of the findings and that way, even if we don't manage to fish up everything, which would be too much to hope for, at least we can make up a little for the disaster."

It all seemed so simple to her and almost already accomplished. She laughed and started fidgeting around. Her despair had suddenly vanished like a bad dream upon waking up.

Just then the valet came in carrying two lamps that he put on the mantle. "Monsieur," he said to the doctor, "Baron Tasimoura."

He did not even have time to finish his sentence. A squalid, scruffy, hideous being in rags, his face covered by a sheet with two eyeholes cut out of it, followed him in and stood before Aristide Cordat.

Spiridon! It was Spiridon in person! And in what a state, good gods, not to speak of his gloomy hood! He was half-dressed in old cotton pants that were too long for him, a torn work shirt and a holey hat, or better to say patched up; from head to foot in nameless rags looking like some morgue worker dressed in a hurry and tied up with shoestrings. He showed up all of a sudden like a ghost barely come out of the shadows and under the lamps brought by the valet he was blinking like an owl in a glittering bedroom.

"Spiridon! At last! Where the devil did you come from dressed like that?" the doctor cried out, caught off guard by the sudden entrance.

"*La Bestia*! *Eccola*!" Pia pronounced almost at the same time, like an echo, and she stood up in front of the apparition.

She did not have time to let her emotions run wild, whatever they might be. Warned by her cry the doctor moved quickly and jumped toward the newcomer. He dragged him to his office, pushed him in and locked the door. Then he rang the bell and gave orders to take Baselli and his daughter to their rooms to wait for his instructions. Finally, he went back to Spiridon, took his pulse and through their usual mental communication asked him, "Where have you come from? You don't look well at all."

"I'll tell you everything, but first give me something to eat. I'm dying of hunger and ready to collapse from weakness," the giant ant answered in the same language and he flopped into a chair that welcomed him with open arms.

The doctor quickly rang the bell again to give orders to serve the baron in the office and told the valet to give his excuses to his guests whom he would see again as soon as possible. For the moment, he was busy with urgent business and could not be disturbed under any circumstances.

And Spiridon threw himself at his rice pudding like a wolf and swallowed glass after glass of good wine. He seemed literally starved and did not even take the time to use his mandibles—he just swallowed whatever was put in front of him. At that rate he was soon filled up and after getting back some strength, he said he was ready to give the explanations that the doctor was impatient for.

From his assistant's first words, Aristide was riveted.

"I thought so!" he said aloud to himself. "Or rather, I knew it! Joel's the one behind it. He was devoured by curiosity and wanted to get to the bottom of things."

Spiridon continued his mental tale with no emotion or anger. He told how he had visited the Dupuytren Museum where the secretary asked him about a will and then made him sign a commitment to the Mutual Autopsy Society to be the executor for his heirs, which he found funny because he did not have any heirs yet, at least not in Paris. Then he went with Le Berquin to his prosector's office. Afterward he explained how the torturer suddenly threw himself on him almost right away, chloroformed him and stripped him of his armor; and how he regained consciousness after who knows how long, but obviously a long time, and was alone, chilly and shivering in the dark on a metal table. He told about Joel's morning visit and his threats on the blackboard.

Finally, he came to the end of his telegraphic story. "A little before noon, when Joel Le Berquin was supposed to come back, the key turned in the lock and a man appeared." (Spiridon summed him up: a bony giant, dressed in a gray sheet over a wool suit with a leather cap above drunken eyes and a thick, gray beard).

"Alcide! The morgue worker, who's responsible for the bodies stored at the Ecole Pratique!" Cordat told himself when he heard this.

"This man," Spiridon continued, "seemed preoccupied. Without saying a word he looked in a rat hole at the bottom of the wall to the left of my table and ended up taking out a leather pouch from which he got two silver coins. He still hadn't noticed me, but kept himself busy with his task. I struggled violently under my straps trying one last time to break them and he finally lifted up his head and saw what he had first thought was a cadaver, but was now struggling in vain on its deathbed. "What's this?" he seemed to say as he got up and came over to me. As I couldn't explain it to him I kept jerking desperately at the straps. The stranger was clearly stunned by what he saw. His 'subjects' never usually gave him such signs of continual vitality. For a minute he stood still there over the table as if he was trying to explain to himself such an abnormal phenomenon. Then when he saw that I wasn't answering him and that I didn't even seem to understand him, as I kept trying to free myself from my bindings, he went slowly, almost automatically, to the shelf where two or three scalpels were lying. He came back to me and cut my straps. As soon as I was freed I jumped to the ground, went to the chalkboard, erased the two lines that were still there and wrote at once:

I'm being held prisoner here through a foul betrayal. 1,000 francs for you, whoever you are, to free me!

"The man looked even more stunned than he was, if that's possible. He moved his lips as if he was talking to me. But seeing that I didn't hear him, he seemed reassured, as if this fact gave him the key to his mistake, to his confusing me with a corpse. And then he took his turn with the chalk. After erasing what I'd written he wrote:

Who brought you here and where do you come from? I'm sure I didn't bring you in my wagon.

"I had to be careful. This busy brute was obviously Joel's henchman since he was the head of employment and absolute master at the Ecole Pratique. I just answered on the board:

I live on Avenue du Bois de Boulogne at the house of Doctor Cordat. 2,000 francs if you get me some clothes and a cab to take me home.

"Answer with chalk:

I'll gladly do it, but after my shift at 5 p.m. For now I can't leave the school.

"I told myself that in the end the solution offered by the stranger was probably the wisest because I surely couldn't appear as I was without causing a scandal and his cooperation was necessary to get me out of there. So, I wrote:

OK. Be here at 5 with some clothes or sheets for me to wear and bring a cab. I repeat: 2000 francs.

"He left and closed the door behind him. I was alone. My first thought was to examine the bottles left on the table by my attacker. One of these bottles was half full of chloroform. The sheet that Le Berquin had used the night before to capture me was still draped over the back of the chair in front of the table.

"I took everything and stood behind the door so that I would be hidden when it opened. And I waited... I did not wait long. Barely 15 minutes after the morgue worker left, I heard that scratching in the lock of the door that I was standing behind. Joel came into the room.

"Before he even had time to notice that I was not where he had left me to spend the harrowing night, his head was covered with the chloroform sheet that I had ready. I wrestled him to the ground while rolling him in the sheet and soaked it with anesthesia. He was under my knees and held down in my grip that was increased tenfold by rage and I shoved the sheet in his mouth. He tried in vain to fight against me. My strength was worn out by anger and his was paralyzed by surprise. After a few seconds I felt his muscles relax in my victorious grasp. He was breathing heavily, already asleep under the cloth. I locked the door again and then I lifted up the sluggish body that was lying motionless at my feet. I heaved it onto the dissection table like he had done to me the night before and emptied the rest of the bottle in his face through the sheet. Then I was out of danger. It was a long day, I admit, but night was finally coming. At 5 p.m. Alcide (he told me his name while helping to disguise me as best as he could in these rags) was on time as agreed. A cab was waiting for me in front of the gate, which was still wide open. He got in with me and gave the address to the coachman who brought us here. And I think the cab is still waiting in the street. Would you like to see Alcide?"

"There's no reason, but obviously you would like him to get paid?"

"Of course. I have nothing but praise for his services and his punctuality."

"You were lucky to escape his clutches! Do you know what people accused this illustrious Alcide of when I went to the Ecole? They claimed that during the siege of Paris in 1870, while he was just an apprentice in the anatomy wing, every night he boiled the waste in a potful of bones to extract the fat and sell it to an old French fry maker on the corner of Rue Antoine Dubois, whom I'm very familiar with. They even started a legal investigation into the matter, but they gave it up because they didn't have enough evidence or maybe they didn't want to outrage the public. I have to admit that the anecdote is not far-fetched. The survivors of the time say that sewer rat stew was a delicacy. It would be surprising that a man as devoid of prejudice as the famous Alcide didn't think of using human fat since he had plenty of it at his disposal. After all, maybe it was patriotism on his part, seeing that he prolonged the resistance!"

Aristide got up and opened one of his desk drawers. He took two bills and sent the valet to give them to the huge morgue worker who was sleeping in the cab while waiting for news from his protégé. The servant had orders to tell him that Doctor Cordat thanked him for taking care of Baron Tasimoura whom he was happy to see safe and sound. After that the carriage door was shut and the horse trotted off.

However, after Aristide had paid the debt of his assistant and collaborator, he lit a cigar, took Spiridon's hand and said to him causally, "You haven't explained what happened to Joel Le Berquin and how you managed with Alcide to avoid any trouble that would necessarily result from his lying on the dissection table."

9. The Prodigal Son

Spiridon looked a little surprised at Aristide's unexpected question, but he answered as if it was, in his view, only of secondary importance.

"Le Berquin?" he said coming out of the dream in which the recent memories seemed to have plunged him. "I strapped him down and covered him with a sheet, so that Alcide could not tell that it was my attacker and not me on the table."

"So you kept him there sleeping the whole time? That must have been around five hours."

"Sleeping? Not at all. What for? I would never have got out of there. *I cut him open, gutted him and dissected him with his own instruments to be sure that he would never bother me again.*"

"Cut open, gutted and dissected?" the doctor repeated hoarsely, forgetting for a second that his partner could not hear him and he added unconsciously, "What? You dared to perpetrate such an attack!" He came back to reality almost instantly and it took a truly superhuman effort for him take the giant ant's hand again and spell out these words because he felt decimated by disgust. "That's unthinkable! You disgust me! I can't believe that you committed such an atrocious crime!"

"Why not believe it?" the so-called Tungus answered coldly. "It's the truth and I don't have to keep it a secret. It would all have started over again if I'd hesitated for a moment. Did the old boy hesitate to lure me into his den under friendly pretexts to anaesthetize me? Did he hesitate to attack me, strip me first of clothes and then of my artificial limbs? Didn't he leave me naked, shivering and hungry in his workshop where he held me hostage? Didn't he want to find out my secrets...and yours...with death threats? And do you doubt that if he'd had the time and energy he would have hesitated to carry out this threat rather than be caught red-handed in theft and kidnapping? As for me, I am absolutely certain about it: if I hadn't got rid of Le Berquin before he had the opportunity to accomplish his ingenious plans, he would have started all over again to torture and starve me in order to extort the valuable information that he meant to have, which you don't even have yet. And he would have ended up cutting my throat to keep the mystery to himself alone. Tell me it's not true, if you dare! And now, instead of being here in this office telling you my adventures, I would be cut into pieces in the cellar of corpses at the Ecole Pratique. Or I'd end up in the bone stew of the famous Alcide, the good man to whom I owe my life, for a fee, and whose job down there is to provide skeletons to the shops around the Ecole, since he doesn't stock the French fry sellers' pots on Rue Antoine Dubois with human fat anymore! If it means anything to you, I still prefer to be here," Spiridon expressed this last thought in his own inimitable way with something like a snicker in his mandibles.

"Brute!" Aristide fumed after sitting there at first, knocked senseless by the terrible revelation. "You have no idea what atrocity you've committed and what a dreadful situation you've put me in. The young man, my fellow student, my friend and colleague—ripped open in cold blood, gutted and dissected in his own workroom at the Ecole, where he earned his position through a competitive exam—on the field of honor you might say—because you figured he had some kind of sinister plan when he probably acted only out of purely scientific curiosity, which is forgivable! It's awful, dreadful! Do you really have no idea of right and wrong? Don't you know that in a civilized society you can't make an attempt on people's lives, even if you believe, rightly or wrongly, that you have good cause? Don't you have any idea of the responsibilities that are imposed on you in your special situation living under my roof? You can't pretend not to see that it's me and me alone that they will accuse, and rightly so...of letting you run wild in the city when you don't have the appearance, education or general principles of humanity. Maybe—I really hope—you are not responsible for your actions, like a mad dog, but I never should have left you alone on the streets to follow your bloody instincts because now I am to blame for your abominations!"

Spiridon remained calm under this avalanche of mute reproach. "I have only one thing to say to you," he answered in his way. "It's that Joel Le Berquin really should have come to you rather than me to find out the secret of your work. He could have easily lured you in person to the school of anatomy, put you to sleep, bound you to the table, tortured you and made you talk before cutting you open. You wouldn't be dead and Joel would have the upper hand! Then, maybe, if you could figure out how to get out of it, you would be right to think as you do. But, since you didn't suffer the experience, you don't have the right! And again, what can I say when I think of what was done to me and how narrowly I escaped...do you know what would have happened to you if Joel had succeeded in his project? He would have made me disappear with no problem at all of course! The cellar of corpses was ready. He only had to give the word to Alcide to put me with the others in unrecognizable bits and pieces. No one would have known a thing.

You yourself would have been the first to think that I left on some whim for some imaginary country. But Joel would not have stopped there! In his greed for our secret, tomorrow or this very evening he would have become forced to kill you too in desperation in order to keep the secret and exploit it alone and escape any suspicions and avoid any future investigation. Your disappearance would be necessary. He would have seen that clearly. He would have been crushed under the weight of evidence and tonight or tomorrow or a little later he would come here, whenever he felt like it, like he used to—and be sure of it, he would have killed you just like me because it's logical and necessary and because the first action would make no sense and be of no importance without the second. That's what you should be telling yourself if you have even the most basic idea of how things work."

"What do I care about your conjectures? There are the facts, miserable insect, that condemn you and disgust me! We're not going to think about what Le Berquin might or might not have done. We're talking about *what you did* and how much horror you are capable of."

"It was a case of legitimate self-defense and I had no other way of escaping the horrible torture!"

"You're telling me this story? Me, who you once treated like you just treated Joel Le Berquin?"

"I didn't know you! It was for my anatomical studies. You were just a subject to me…"

"Like the one I saw in your underground lab on the table next to mine? Thanks for clearing that up. It helps me know what I have to do as I learn about your sense of morality. You are and will always be just a brutal beast, beyond any help to tell the difference between good and evil, just following your instincts automatically. That's your excuse, I suppose. But that's also what makes it unforgivable for me to let you continue what you're doing. You can't stay free and do whatever your rudimentary brain tells you to do. You're a public danger, especially for my honor and my security. From now on I can't share the responsibility of your actions!"

"You're happy enough to share the benefits of my hereditary treasure and my work! That's great. I know what I have to do."

"I can say the same. But first of all I have to keep you from doing any more evil by locking you up like the dangerous animal you are until further notice."

The doctor rang the bell and summoned all the men of the house. They came running and lined up in front of the office door.

"Baron Tasimoura is under criminal investigation," he told them. "Take him to his room, lock him in and keep a close watch until you hear from me!"

Left alone, Aristide Cordat collapsed into his armchair to consider the terrible problem that he faced. What should he do? What action should he take in the bloody tragedy that he was mixed up in because of the wretched creature whom he had torn away from his studious solitude to throw into the middle of civilization where he wreaked havoc on the fly? Yesterday: Pia's brother's throat cut and himself undergoing the start of a dissection; Pia paralyzed at the entrance of the grotto; Baselli and his helpers threatened with the same fate. And today: Joel Le Berquin disemboweled in the middle of medical school at the Ecole Pratique! That was the sticky point that he had to deal with immediately. The horrible murder, which was still completely unknown, was going to be the talk of Paris and the rest of the world in a few hours. He had to explain it and make the public understand. It was not only the perpetrator's life that was at stake, but the honor of the one who brought the murderer into France and made him his collaborator and assistant and whom everyone was surely going to accuse of direct or indirect involvement in the unheard-of crime. But putting aside such an eventuality, he still had to vindicate himself and do so without saying too much about the giant ant or about where he came from or his secret inheritance. This was a terribly agonizing problem for a young, eager man like Aristide, who found himself suddenly shot into the limelight and whom such revelations threatened to pull down from his glory, forever.

For a minute he thought of cutting off the evil at its root in collusion with Alcide, the old mortician at the Ecole Pratique, to get rid of the physical evidence. Alcide could do it easily. He was not an incorruptible man. He was the only one with a key to Joel's office and could enter whenever he wanted without raising any suspicions. Nothing could be easier and more normal for a man in his position to pile up human remains in his wagon and bring them to the crematorium. He did it every day. Even without making him a conscious collaborator, maybe it was possible to work it out without his knowing, either by preparing him with drinks at the right time or by sorting the disfigured remains into different tubs in the dissection rooms. All this was feasible, of course, and even relatively easy for someone who knew the practices of the anatomy school. And it would take care of everything, *forever*! Joel disappeared, that's the fact. Aristide himself had just taken some official steps, in a way, to find some clue to his whereabouts, with no results. The police detectives were following up on the disappearance with the evidence he provided them. They would never think of searching for him in Alcide's mortuary storeroom or in his wagon or in the oven at Père Lachaise cemetery! Even if they came up with such an idea, the remains of the dead man would be unrecognizable at first and then gone up in smoke within an hour...

The plan of action grew in Doctor Cordat's imagination for a few minutes with such force that he needed all his strength to push it away. It was simple: it was easy to do and sure. And he would destroy in one fell swoop all the harmful consequences that the disclosure of the murder had to bring with it. In the end it seemed ever more tempting because Aristide really had no responsibility in the crime and thought only of automatically erasing, if you could say that, the disastrous consequences that might affect Spiridon and himself.

He had the moral courage to resist this temptation and chase it away like a bad dream. He stood up suddenly. "No! Come what may, it will not be said that I backed down from my basic duty! And this duty is to notify the legal authorities right away of what happened, since they are already informed about the beginning of the tragedy."

He called for his automobile and went to look for the Chief of Police. It was 8 p.m.

Aristide Cordat did not find the magistrate at his office and had to wait for him. But when he explained to the detective on duty that it was a serious matter, *urgent*, and that it was necessary to call the high official on the phone to tell him that he was needed in person, Monsieur Brideau did not keep him waiting long. Still, it was almost 9 p.m. when he arrived and his unintentional bad mood was not very well hidden behind his flushed face and red cat whiskers.

"I was having dinner with friends," he said as an introduction, "but we don't have the right to eat dinner in this damn job! Your voice was all it took to drag me away from the sweet desserts. Anyway, I hope it's not for nothing. Have you found your friend in a delicate situation?" he asked as he came in without the strength to give up his cigar.

"Ah! I've brought you glum news."

"You found him hurt? Maybe dead?"

"No, Chief, Sir, he came back alone, half-naked, in rags, after facing the darkest dangers. But what made me run to you is the dismal news I have about Doctor Le Berquin. I asked you this afternoon to investigate…"

"We were on it right away. Two of my sharpest detectives followed the clues you gave. They went everywhere Doctor Le Berquin usually goes. They hadn't seen him for two days at his office on Rue Hautefeuille. At the Hôtel-Dieu Hospital they saw him at the clinic this very morning. At the Ecole Pratique the gatekeeper spoke to him around noon. The circumstances seem reassuring according to my detectives' reports."

"Monsieur, Doctor Le Berquin is lying dead, with his guts and brain removed, on a dissection table in his workshop at the Ecole Pratique."

"It's not possible! Have you seen him with your own eyes?"

"Unfortunately I have no reason to doubt it and I come to you to ask to make a statement right away."

"We'll do it in the anatomy room."

The Chief of Police rang a bell and his secretary came in. "Four men from the Special Crime Squad with a sergeant and two wagons! And get a third one for the doctor and me!"

"I have my car and can offer you a ride, as well as the gentleman if he's coming with us."

"Thank you. Like that we can talk on the way. If you want, we can leave without waiting for the men. They'll follow us. (To his secretary) Give orders to go to the Ecole Pratique, Rue de Ecole de Medecine at the end of Rue Hautefeuille, and wait for me in the courtyard of the museum. (To the doctor) Whenever you're ready."

They went down the stairs, found the automobile waiting at the sidewalk and got on their way.

They had barely left when the Chief of Police said, "I won't ask you if you have any theories about the death we're going to see, but if you do, I don't have to tell you that I would be very glad to hear them."

"I have not only a theory about it, but a certainty," Aristide replied. "I will give it to you such as it is after making sure it's true, but you understand my reservations given the extreme gravity of the situation. I haven't seen Doctor Le Berquin's corpse with my own eyes and I'm still hoping, in spite of everything…maybe there will still be time to save him."

The car had already crossed over the Saint Michel Bridge and went up the boulevard of the same name. It turned onto Rue Ecole de Medecine and stopped in front of the gate of the Ecole Pratique. The doctor was about to ring for the gatekeeper, but the policeman held him back.

"Hold on a minute, please! This is my business."

He rang the bell so loud and clear that the whole courtyard of Cordeliers echoed. The gatekeeper showed up, clearly angry.

"Who's ringing like that? Have you ever seen such a ruckus?" he screamed, apparently talking about the students gathering around.

A deep voice answered him, "In the name of the law! The Chief of Police!"

Through the gate the guard saw the sash that the Chief held out. He rushed to open up and apologized profusely.

"You have Doctor Le Berquin here, prosector of the school?"

"The prosector has a laboratory in the building to the left, but he's usually not here at this hour. They already came to ask me this evening after he'd left. I told them that I hadn't seen him since noon."

"I know that. The detectives came here for me. Take us to his laboratory. Do you have the key?"

"Yes, Captain, or at least I'm supposed to have it. But I think I left it with Alcide, the morgue worker, and he's not here."

"It doesn't matter. Do you have a crow bar or something to break the door open?"

"Oh, sure! The bar for the sewer plate will do the job."

"Very well. Light a lantern or a torch, get the bar and show me the way."

The man in his trimmed uniform hurried to obey. He did not have a lantern, but lit a brass candlestick, took the bar from the back of the kitchen and led the two visitors toward the buildings that opened onto the courtyard. When they got to the door, another ringing of the bell, as authoritative as the first, surprised him.

"That would be the special agents who are joining me," the Chief said. "Have them bring the wagons into the courtyard and tell them to wait for me. Then come back and show me the way."

The errand took a few minutes and attracted the attention of the passers-by on the street. A group of gawkers gathered in front of the gate, which the gatekeeper closed on them and locked with a key before rejoining the Chief of Police.

"Now let's go!" he said.

"Do you suspect an accident or a crime?" the guardian asked since his curiosity was piqued by the events.

"There's reason to believe that Doctor Le Berquin has been murdered in his laboratory," the magistrate answered.

"Doctor Le Berquin? Impossible. I'm sure I saw him around noon."

"Did you see him enter or leave?"

"Enter, of course! It was exactly when I was about to have lunch with my wife."

"Well, we are going to get to the bottom of this. Is that the door to his lab?"

"Yes, sir."

"It doesn't look very solid. We won't be needing your bar."

On saying this the Chief of Police took a step back, gathered his strength and like a professional he kicked open the door, which swung in as he had figured.

"Come on, the candle, right now! So, you don't have gas in this box?"

"Excuse me, Captain. It just has to be turned on over by the stove."

"Well, turn it on right away and we'll proceed with the examination."

At first sight nothing seemed out of place in the prosector's office, at least nothing that you wouldn't expect to find in such a place. On the table to the right a sheet vaguely outlined the contours of a corpse. That was nothing shocking in itself; the precaution could even be considered more decent than usual in the schools of anatomy. The magistrate went up to the table, lifted the sheet and threw it on the ground. A disemboweled body, opened down the median line from chest to belly, was lying there.

Not only were the internal organs of the body removed (lungs, heart, liver, stomach and intestines), but the orbits were missing their eyeballs and the skull, which had been sawn across the supraorbital ridge, had been emptied of the brain. All these pieces were piled up on the table in a soft, bloody heap between the dead man's legs. One of the eyes seemed to be watching them out of the liver. While the witnesses of this macabre confirmation were leaning over the face to try to recognize it, the gatekeeper, who was not yet hardened to this kind of sight, suddenly collapsed and fell flat on the tile floor.

"There goes our main witness," the Chief remarked, otherwise unmoved. "But I'm sure you'd recognize the deceased, Doctor. Do you think it's him?"

"There's not a shadow of a doubt!" Aristide Cordat affirmed. "The shape of the face, the forehead, nose, chin...not to mention the body that I recognize well enough since I went swimming with him. The hair, hands, beard...everything tells me that we have before us the remains of Joel Le Berquin. And I can say that the way the poor man's corpse is arranged is like the murderer's signature."

"Exactly what I was thinking! He's a medical man, isn't he? A doctor? An anatomist?"

"Well, yes. A quasi-anatomist, at the very least, with enough practice to carve someone up as elaborately as we see here."

Just then the two men remembered the poor gatekeeper, still lying on the ground, groaning and fidgeting.

"We can't just leave the poor man like this," Aristide said as he bent down to take his pulse. "If you'd like, Chief, I could take him back to his place."

"Don't bother! I'll call for the detectives in the courtyard," the Chief of Police responded.

He took the time to put the sheet he had thrown aside back on the dissection table and then headed for the door to the courtyard. He called out for two of his men who came right away to lift up the gatekeeper and carry him to his home.

"Tell his wife not to worry," the doctor told them. "He just fainted and will come out of it soon, probably on the way over. She should give him some tea with a little rum or cognac. And I'll drop by later to see how he's doing...Doctor Cordat!" he added for their information.

And turning to the Chief of Police, "Do we stay here or go somewhere else to talk?"

"Whatever you want. The important thing for me now is to make a report and ask you to act as a witness so I can send it immediately to the Prosecutor's Office. And if you want to tell me what you know about all this, it would make it much easier for me to pursue my investigation."

"Well, let's go to the gatekeeper's house. At least it'll be more comfortable there for what we have to do."

The two men went back to the outside courtyard where the Chief of Police ordered one of his detectives to go and find a locksmith to close the door of the laboratory, which also had to be guarded until further notice. Then he joined the doctor in the rooms of the gatekeeper whose wife had already put him to bed after he came to.

"You understand that I kind of collapsed when I recognized that poor Monsieur Le Berquin?" he said between two gulps of rum tea. "An old soldier like me! I've seen all kinds of things in Algeria and China, but finding him on that table...the Ecole's prosector who I saw fresh as a daisy at this very gate this afternoon at noon... It was so unexpected that my blood rushed to my head."

"So, you, too, recognized him. And you're sure about his identity?" the Chief of Police asked, coming in the middle of the conversation.

"Oh, Captain, there's not a shadow of a doubt. It was the face, beard, hair and everything that looked like Monsieur Le Berquin."

"Well, I'll make a report of all this right now," the magistrate said, "sitting down at the desk and taking out of his briefcase the duly stamped papers that he carried with him whenever his presence was required.

It only took a few minutes. The report included the verbal petition of Doctor Aristide Cordat, the "canvassing" carried out by the Chief of Police, the discovery of the corpse in the building of the Ecole Pratique, on a dissection table, totally naked, with innards and brain removed, of a man around 30 years old whom Doctor Aristide Cordat (present at the scene) said he recognized as being Doctor Joel Le Berquin, prosector of the School of Medicine, who lived in Paris, 81 Rue Hautefeuille, where the doorman of the building had stated that he had not seen him since the night before and the gatekeeper at the Ecole Pratique also stated that he had seen him enter that morning around noon. This same guard, moreover, stated that no one to his knowledge had entered the prosector's building except the students of the said prosector or, by chance, a student from another building and for his duties the morgue worker Alcide Janiaux, who takes care of the mortuary storeroom and the delivery wagon of the anatomy school. There followed a brief description of the condition of the corpse, the mutilations it had suffered and the probable time it took to perform these mutilations. In testimony of this the Chief of Police signed his name and official capacity and provided the signatures of the two witnesses present at his raid on the place, Doctor Aristide Cordat, ex-intern at hospitals in Paris, residing at 187 Avenue Bois de Boulogne, and Monsieur Jean Louis Castiras, ex-noncommissioned engineer officer, decorated with the Médaille Militaire, guard and gatekeeper at the school of Medicine of the Ecole Pratique.

When the document was duly concluded and signed, Doctor Cordat and the Chief of Police said goodbye to the gatekeeper and his wife and headed for the waiting automobile.

"Where would you like me to take you?" the doctor asked the magistrate.

"To the Palais de Justice if you could," he answered. "I insist on notifying the Public Prosecutor about this as soon as possible."

"Will he be in his office?"

"Certainly not at this hour, or at least it's very unlikely. But there's always someone there and they can get him on the phone and tell him that I'm ready for whenever he's available."

"Do you think that I can come with you to see him? I have a sensitive matter to discuss with him and would like to get it off my chest so that I don't have to go back over all the miserable details of this tragedy. Besides, I have to admit that I wouldn't mind having dinner somewhere, anywhere, since my stomach is as empty as a hollow shell, as they say."

"Well, let's see what we can do. I'll forward your request to the Public Prosecutor on the telephone. You go get dinner and leave me the address. I'll get the Prosecutor's answer to you where you tell me to."

"Just go to Foyot. I'll go there after I drop you off and send the car back to make it easier for you to find me quickly when you get the answer."

And so it was agreed. Doctor Cordat left the Chief of Police at the door of the Prosecutor's Office, went to the restaurant that he had said he would go to and sent back his automobile to be at the magistrate's disposal.

The Chief did not take long. It was almost 11 p.m. when he joined Doctor Cordat enjoying his dinner in a little dining room.

"The Prosecutor is waiting for us at his home on Rue de la Boëtie," he said when he entered. "I would have joined you earlier, but I thought that you wouldn't mind taking your time to eat. And besides, I had to go see my boss to tell him what's happening. He fully approved of my actions and told me to tell you that he would like to see you tomorrow in his office or somewhere else, if you can spare a few minutes."

"No problem. Tomorrow morning I will go to his office. Now, if you'd like, we can go to Rue de la Boëtie."

The Public Prosecutor, Monsieur Jordan, was waiting for his visitors in a very simple office on the second floor. He was around 50 years old, thin and dry, with graying hair and gold glasses and was dressed formally. He welcomed Doctor Cordat with respect that was clearly in homage to his very recent accomplishments; and he greeted the Chief of Police with a kind of professional familiarity. He put the young man at ease right away.

"You wanted to speak with me about the events at the Ecole Pratique that the Chief of Police filled me in on over the telephone. Your time is precious, I know. I thought that it would be better to hear you out this evening because I have no doubts about the gravity of the motive that must be compelling you. That's why I left the Ministry of Justice to come listen to you."

Aristide Cordat bowed.

"What I have to tell you is a very delicate matter, indeed, and that's why I thought I should ask to see you right away, Monsieur Prosecutor. It's not only delicate, but more than that it's painful. I know who Joel Le Berquin's murderer is. I know the extraordinary circumstances surrounding the murder and I insist on explaining everything without delay. Moreover, I really want to keep the police from following false leads and wandering onto the wrong track. That would put them in a dangerous situation—I mean a ridiculous situation. Excuse me for using such an expression, which is maybe a little hard, but the preventative steps that I think are urgent and necessary will show that I mean no offense to anyone."

The prosecutor made a sign of approval and the doctor gave his account.

He explained all the particular circumstances that brought him to know the truth about the murder and the revolting details that the prosector of the School of Medicine was the victim of. Doctor Joel Le Berquin was a schoolmate and a personal friend, the only one whom he found necessary to invite to his recent operations in front of a very limited audience of experts—operations that the Public Prosecutor had no doubt heard of because the newspapers had been full of them for the last two weeks. He thought he owed this exceptional respect to an already old friendship between him and the deceased, as well as to the disappointment the friend felt recently when he was unable to go with the witness (as had been agreed) on a sea voyage that they were supposed to take together. Unfortunately the deceased was ambitious and jealous. Instead of feeling glad to have seen these crucial experiments—alone among his generation—he was offended by the secrets that the experimenter thought he had to keep quiet about temporarily, as well as the nature of the chemical products used to perform what looked like a real surgical miracle. So, unfortunately he tried to steal the secrets that could not be revealed right away and with this in mind he came to the house on Avenue du Bois with prying eyes, which was often just like spying. Two of three times the witness was sorry to have caught his friend red-handed breaking his trust, even when they were alone. But he was not particularly upset because he knew that the attempts were useless. He was even a little amused by them. But he certainly regretted it bitterly because they ended up driving Doctor Le Berquin to commit outright crimes, which became the direct cause of his appalling end.

As Doctor Cordat got to this crucial point in his story, his voice changed noticeably. He finished stammering through and was choked by emotion.

"I'm sure you understand, Monsieur Prosecutor, how painful it is for me to make such an outright accusation—an accusation with the most serious consequences—against a man...a friend...a school chum, just when he's come to such a terrible and premature end as a result of his actions. But I can't escape from this dreadful duty! I have to tell the truth, the whole truth, to keep justice from going on the wrong track, like pursuing the morgue worker Alcide Janiaux, for example, or from winding up in a dead-end. There's a young foreigner who came with me to Paris to be my collaborator and assistant. He doesn't speak our language or any other civilized tongue, but he possesses certain fundamental elements of my work. It'd be better to say that he himself is the starting point and origin of the work. Joel Le Berquin tried in vain to get information from this private partner about the interests that obsessed him. Joel obviously decided to get the details he craved by hook or by crook. Naturally I'm only guessing at this point!

"Still, Joel lured my collaborator into a trap on the pretext of visiting the Dupuytren Museum at the school where he was officially assigned and ended up holding him captive in his personal office. This happened yesterday, Wednesday, between 3 and 5 p.m. I can give you proof of this because I found the coachman who drove my assistant to a glassworks shop and left him with Le Berquin on Rue Monsieur le Prince around that time. From this well-known street in the Latin Quarter, Joel brought him to the Dupuytren Museum next to the Ecole Pratique and then to his laboratory, which the students had just left as night was falling. And there, I am sorry to have to say, alone like he was every evening in the dark solitude, but this time with my assistant, Joel Le Berquin asked his prisoner some hard questions to find out the secrets. Then, seeing that he was getting nowhere playing nice, he suddenly threw a sheet around his enemy's head, held him down and rendered him helpless. He had poured a half bottle of chloroform on the sheet around the nose and mouth, which naturally worked like anesthesia. And then he threw my assistant on a dissection table and bound him tightly with leather straps. He wrote with chalk on the blackboard, threatening that if he didn't reveal what he wanted to know, he would kill him, and then he left the Ecole Pratique for the whole night, leaving the poor hostage to wake up and imagine what was in store."

Here the Public Prosecutor thought he should ask something. "Of course you got these details from the prisoner himself?"

"From the prisoner himself who told me in detail as soon as he could! This very morning Joel came back to repeat his threat, telling the victim that he had to go to Hôtel-Dieu Hospital and would leave him to his thoughts and come back at noon for an answer. Once again he left him to choose either confessing the truth or dying in silence. Then he locked him in again.

"You can easily imagine, Monsieur Prosecutor, what a pitiful state the poor thing was in, bound tightly to the torture table, alone, hungry and separated from the world in that macabre and deserted place. Not only was he unable to do or say anything, but he couldn't even cry out and call for help because he can't speak. It's obvious to me that if his torturer had come back right then, the ill-fated being could have done nothing but give in to the pressure that so cruelly conspired against him. Afterward, to make sure the silence would not be broken, his executioner would not have spared his life, since he had all the means at his disposal. But by undreamed of luck, Tasimoura was able to escape from this abominable threat. A little after noon, just when Le Berquin was supposed to come back and perpetrate his crime—he had no time to lose since in less than an hour his students were going to be crowding into the anatomy building— the morgue worker Alcide Janiaux, well-known in the Ecole, came to get a little money that he'd hidden in a hole in the laboratory wall. He noticed the desperate movement of a living being that he had taken for a corpse on the dissection table. He cut the straps that bound the victim and was persuaded by the promise of a reward to come back after his daily chores with some clothes to replace the ones Le Berquin had cut up. It was agreed that he would complete the rescue by bringing a carriage into the courtyard at nightfall to take the poor victim to his home, which is mine. The negotiation was carried out on the chalkboard.

"Le Berquin was coming back any minute. The morgue worker left and locked the door behind him. Monsieur Prosecutor, I'm coming to the end of the sinister tale. At noon Le Berquin came back as he had said. We told you that the gatekeeper saw him pass by his room and he even spoke to him, not at all suspecting that he was heading to his death. It was lying in wait for him and was going to strike him down in the most unexpected way. He had barely opened the door to his laboratory when a sheet came down over his head—the same sheet he had used the night before in the same way. An unforeseen attacker jumped on him, rolled him on the ground, held him down and drowned him with the chloroform that he had used before. After putting him to sleep and rendering him unconscious like that, he threw him on the table—just like Joel had done to his victim. Oh, he was carried away by a justifiable anger and…he killed him with his own knife, cut him open and took out all his vital organs. In a word, he got his just rewards, without a doubt, but basically it was only the logical conclusion and compensation for a crime that he had planned, begun and half-completed."

10. The Fire

During this emotional story, the Public Prosecutor did not move, as if he was dumbstruck. He broke his silence when Doctor Cordat stopped talking and he asked him, "You got these details from the murderer himself, from your collaborator and assistant?"

"At 7 p.m. he came back in a pitiful state, led by his savior, the morgue worker Alcide. First of all he wanted to pay what he had promised and to eat because he was famished. Then he told me in detail, in the language we are used to communicating in, the story of the 30 hours that he had spent outside my house. And my first thought was that I had to bring this unheard-of drama to court after verifying the facts. That's why I ran to Police Headquarters and went with the Chief of Police to see the state of things at the Ecole Pratique. That's also why I wanted to tell you as soon as possible the specifics of this hideous affair."

"I sincerely thank you, Monsieur, for the care you have taken. As for us, we will carry out our duty." The magistrate turned to the Chief of Police and asked, "The murderer is obviously in holding?"

"Not yet, Monsieur Prosecutor. Doctor Cordat formally swore that he was being kept under watch at his house, which I believe, so I thought we should give you the inside story of these dark dealings first."

"So, there's an inside story? I see very well the motives behind the actions of poor Doctor Le Berquin. And I can understand the desire for vengeance of his adversary...what's his name?"

"Baron Tasimoura."

"Yes, that's the name I saw in the newspapers concerning those wonderful operations. You said he was a foreigner? Where does he come from? Can you tell me something about him? I don't need to tell you that we'll get an arrest warrant against him and put him in the Conciergerie prison."

"Monsieur Prosecutor, that's exactly what will be impossible to do. Baron Tasimoura...Spiridon, to call him by his real name, is not at all responsible. Not only can he not be brought to justice because he can't answer questions or take part in any kind of judicial hearing since he can't hear or speak any articulate language, but also—if we admit that it would be open to the public—it would be kind of revolting and totally disgraceful in a civilized country like ours because Tasimoura or Spiridon, as we should call him, is totally incapable of understanding that he committed a crime, or I should say, that *he did anything wrong*. He is, I repeat, *unaware of any human law*. He is as innocent and irresponsible as a mad dog or a wild horse!"

"Monsieur Doctor, how can you want to make us believe such a statement? A man who so coldly, so knowingly and also so cruelly committed such a thing? And he was your collaborator in those scientific works that just distinguished you? I can say, as you yourself admit, that he was the instigator and true creator of these works! I'm sure the jury will take into consideration the extenuating circumstances of his crime and I will be the first one to bring them to light. But it is impossible, *a priori*, to admit that he committed this crime without knowing what he was doing and without responsibility."

"But it's the truth, Monsieur Prosecutor! You will understand after I tell you the final reason that makes me say this and that will prevent you or anyone else from bringing this irresponsible being to human justice. The reason is imperative: Spiridon, Monsieur Prosecutor, *is not a human being*. He's an animal—a refined insect, a giant ant who managed to develop his instinct to an imperfect intellectual level, but who is still, in spite of everything, an animal, an unaware, irresponsible animal and totally innocent."

Dumbstruck by the revelation, the magistrate said nothing at first, as if knocked out by what he had heard. But very soon he got a hold of himself and stood up before the young doctor.

"If what you are telling me is true and I won't insult you by doubting it, your first duty, Doctor, and in any case mine, is to prove it in public in front of men! I can understand your misgivings and that you want to keep such an unusual creature hidden away, but from now on that will be impossible. Neither you nor I have the right to assume such a responsibility. We can only submit the case to competent experts so that they can make their report. Supposing that this report be in every way favorable to the accused and supposing even that it be upheld by the verdict of a free and mindful jury later on, it will then be our urgent duty to keep this irresponsible, destructive beast out of harm's way! Therefore, my first act will be to have him arrested. Chief, I will sign the warrant immediately and leave it up to you."

Saying this the prosecutor went back to his desk, took an arrest warrant out of the drawer, filled in a few lines and signed it.

"Go on, gentlemen," he said as he gave the paper to the Chief. "I'm sorry, Doctor, to have to take these measures that obviously upset you, but if you could for one minute put yourself in my place, you would see that I have no other choice. Moreover, I need to ask that you be available to the investigating judge whom I will assign to the case. He will probably summons you to his office at the Palais de Justice tomorrow to take your deposition."

With that Doctor Cordat left with the Police Chief, went back to his car and gave orders to go directly to Avenue du Bois.

It was midnight. During the time it took to make the quick trip down Champs Elysées the doctor was silently absorbed in his thoughts. He was the first to see that the Public Prosecutor had to do what he just did. And all things considered, given where things stood—the anger that clearly spurred on Spiridon, the need to put an end to his blind violence and the need to protect him against the vengeful fury of Pia Baselli—the idea of immediately arresting him and handing him over to the expertise of competent men was maybe the best solution, the wisest in any case. He had to be able to give in to circumstances when they were so overwhelming. An open, public examination of Spiridon's mental state could have its advantages, both for the present and the future. Once the fact was established that the giant ant was an insect and nothing but an insect, truly unaware and irresponsible, it might be possible to get some supportive care and protection in a cushy, comfortable imprisonment, as far as possible, and to protect the poor being from his own recklessness, as well as from the fury of others.

Aristide was thinking of such things, sunk down in the corner of his car when the Chief of Police shook him out of his reveries.

"Hey, do you see the sky lit up over l'Etoile?" he asked leaning out of the window. "And all the people crowded around there. There must be a big fire either in Suresnes or Puteaux!"

He lowered the window and talked to the chauffeur. "Stop for a minute, if you see a police officer. We can ask him what's happening."

Almost immediately the car slowed down and stopped in front of an officer who was directing the foot traffic that had suddenly become packed.

"Do you know where the fire is?" the Chief of Police asked.

"Yes, Captain," the officer replied right away, saluting his chief as soon as he recognized him. "It's on Avenue du Bois, at the famous doctor's house. The alarm was given an hour ago. All the firemen of the district are working on it and the Prefect just passed by on his way to the blaze."

The automobile sped up as it left and was stopped at l'Etoile by a row of policemen.

"Where's the fire?" the magistrate asked again.

"At Doctor Cordat's house, end of the street on the left," the sergeant answered.

"I knew it!" Aristide shouted. "I knew it two minutes ago... They're going to let us in, aren't they?"

The Chief of Police identified himself and the car went through after letting the sergeant in next to the chauffeur to make things easy.

The crowd on the street was huge, on both sidewalks and the lawn, on the balconies, in the windows and on the roofs. But the street was clear for the firemen behind the row of police officers. The fire was almost put out. Black smoke was swirling into the sky forming a huge cloud above the gaslights that in the suddenly gloomy scene looked like funeral lamps.

Getting out of the car in front of the barely extinguished blaze, Aristide saw that a large piece of the terrace wall had been broken to let in the firehoses, which were hooked up to all the hydrants in the area and converged in the yard like a bunch of gigantic snakes. Around the pumps the firemen were busy directing torrents of water onto the walls and roofs of the closest houses.

The Chief of Police caught sight of the Prefect in front of the breach and introduced Doctor Cordat.

"It's terribly unfortunate what has happened to you," the Prefect said to him. "Such a beautiful house and full of wonderful things, which won't be entirely lost, we hope. Of course, you're insured, aren't you?"

"I don't even know yet. My architect was in charge of that and I think he probably took the necessary steps. Has anybody been hurt?"

"Two or three of our people. One firefighter was hit in the head by a falling beam and another got a broken arm, but I think that the entire household got out in time. Our men are just now going through the house. They went in as soon as they got the fire under control."

Aristide hurried over to the yard and saw his house staff gathered into a circle under the trees off the terrace. Just then he saw Pia with her father, who was sitting on the lawn and crying.

She looked like a maenad, a wild nymph, and was shaking with tears. She was pale, disheveled and black from the smoke; her hair and eyelashes were burned; her clothes were in rags.

"*Birbante*! *Canaglia*!" she waved around a stiletto, red with blood. "He's the one who started the fire, but I took care of him! He won't kill anyone anymore!" she said as soon as she saw Aristide and she ran toward him.

"Poor girl! What are you rambling about? Who did you hurt?" the doctor asked full of fear and terror.

"Who else but that infernal *bestia*..." she replied with savage honesty, "the one who killed my Orso and wanted to kill us and topped off his crimes by setting your house on fire!"

"What are you talking about, Pia? It looks like..."

"Looks like? Ask anyone here if it's not true. Ask my father who is crying his eyes out and everyone else. You ordered them to guard the *bestia* and it was locked up in its room for two or three hours when suddenly my father and I heard something in the room next to ours while we were waiting for you to come back. We heard a devilish racket. It was the *bestia* who was breaking all the bottles and jars with a hammer. It was hard to figure out what it was doing, but it must have been demonically angry and swinging blindly at everything. The infernal racket went on and on; windows were smashed to bits and crashed to the floor. You'd have thought that 100,000 lost souls were crowding into the room! My father and I went onto the landing wondering what kind of Sabbath was taking place. Everyone else was already on the stairs, terrified. And then a flood of smoking liquid that burned everything started pouring out from under the villain's door and soon spilled onto the landing. It flowed down the stairs, devoured the carpet, flared up all by itself and looked like it was going to burn everything. The terrified staff ran away yelling fire. They fled into the street asking for help. I could still hear the *bestia* continuing its villain's work, breaking and smashing everything. Then I grabbed an axe that was nearby in the glass room and I chopped at the door with more strength than I thought I had. I broke through the lock and saw it, standing in the middle of an unsightly mess on top of a pile of glass and wood with its feet covered by a fuming pool. The hideous *bestia* kept going at it. With all my strength I hit it over the head with the axe and it fell to the floor. It rolled around in the wreckage and the flood of acid rushed to the stairs. I barely had time to stab the *bestia* in the eyes with my stiletto before I ran away because everything was catching on fire with the wind from the stairs. My hair and eyelashes were already half-burnt. But it's all over now, *caro signore*! The *bestia* won't hurt anyone! It's dead and gone for good—like I wanted, like I swore!"

Saying this Pia got up in her big shoes that were red from the acid and stood there righteously proud of her deed.

Aristide's desperate bitterness brought him back to reality.

"Poor girl, what have you done?" he said, wringing his hands. "After destroying the castle and its treasure you had to come here to sacrifice the possessor of the most precious secrets? So, it was an inescapable fate! And you had to prove yourself by a disaster that will destroy everything, even my honor, because they're going to accuse me of killing the witness and real creator of my works! Oh, cursed vendetta, cursed day, curse on your meddling in things that you don't understand, that you cannot even suspect! But maybe it's not all lost. Maybe the poor creature isn't dead. I have to find out right away. That's my first and foremost duty."

He turned away from the helpless group of servants and ran toward the Prefect to tell him about this new disaster.

"I just got some dreadful news and I can't even say what the impact will be!" he panted. "My collaborator and helper, Tasimoura…Spiridon…who admitted killing the prosector of the Ecole Pratique in the pressing danger he was thrown in…Tasimoura should be found upstairs in his laboratory and, apparently, he has died there after starting the fire with acids and other chemicals that he smashed with a hammer. We'll have to check now to see if there's not some life left in him...right away...right now!"

The Prefect turned to the firemen and gave them some quick orders. Within 20 seconds the iron ladder was set up and rolling toward the windows that Aristide pointed out. The first rung barely touched the balcony before the young doctor rushed up, closely followed by the firemen, the Prefect and the Chief of Police.

One after another they quickly scaled the iron bars and climbed onto the third-floor balcony. They ran straight for the laboratory among the smoking ruins. Aristide got there first...or so he thought...

The grim scene he found was not what he was expecting.

Terrified by his scolding, Pia had dashed to the crumbling staircase just when they were rolling out the ladder. She got there before everyone and stabbed herself in the heart on top of Spiridon's corpse.

Her father had followed close behind her tragic ascent and seen her die at his feet. He went crazy with grief just when the crowd of rescuers came through the window. He dove headfirst over the railing of the marble staircase and broke his neck on the ground floor.

The others rushed to the two victims in the laboratory, one already dead and the other dying. Pia was still breathing.

One of the firemen picked her up in his arms and another picked up the fragile remains of Spiridon. Then the whole group filed down the ladder as quickly as they had come up.

Pia came to for a brief moment on the grass outside where they laid her down. She opened her eyes and stared at the doctor who was kneeling next to her and dabbing her forehead with eau-de-vie. When she saw him, something like a peaceful smile passed over her paling face.

"*Addio, caro dottore. Disgraziata io...mori per l'amor di Vostra signoria...e del fratello! Mori vindicata!*"[6]

There was no telling which was more sorrowful in the double expression of two loves that had taken seed in that simple heart and merged—the love of her brother or of the distant hero who had suddenly come into her life to light it up with a ray of glory and tenderness.

All of a sudden her head fell back on the lawn. She was dead.

Aristide was moved by her sublime sacrifice that revealed an unsuspected affection. He leaned over her sorrowful face and kissed her goodbye for himself and for Orso. Then he stood up as the firemen were bringing over her father's body from the foot of the marble stairs with his head crushed.

He had to face all this and somehow explain this sequel to the drama. The Prefect and the Chief of Police were already coming over to the firemen gathered around the bodies to proceed with their investigation by getting statements from the house staff.

One after another told what they had seen, how the fire had broken out. They each told how the old Sardinian fisherman and his daughter had come from Genoa that very day. They told of the Baron's return and being

---

[6] Farewell, dear Doctor. Cursed be me...I die for love of you...and my brother! I die avenged!

held in custody in his room while the doctor ran off to the Boulevard du Palais; then the baron's silent fury, smashing all the glass in the laboratory with a hammer, the rapid flood and the fire.

From the facts and the sometimes childish details that were given in the first wave of emotions by all the witnesses of the disaster, the striking but still rough truth finally came out: the total innocence and sincerity of Doctor Cordat, his desperate measures to find Le Berquin and Spiridon and notify the police, the loss of hope and the ruin of his work he suffered just after his glorious debut through this incredible sequence of deaths, hatred, jealousy and ambition...

"My dear Doctor, you should go lie down," the Prefect said when he had finished his summary investigation. "The dead will be taken to the City Morgue with the remains of Joel Le Berquin. We can finish this sad tale tomorrow. But do you know where you can go for some much-needed rest? Would you like to stay with me?"

"Thank you, but I still have a temporary apartment I left only three weeks ago and I and my staff can stay there. Needless to say you can call on me anytime."

The Prefect left while the wagons were coming to take the victims away.

And then Aristide Cordat thought about the poor beings who had worked for him and appreciated him and so soon after meeting him had to suffer through such tragic events. He did not want them to go alone to the last refuge of Parisian miseries where they had come from to share a roof together. He had his automobile brought up and followed their convoy all the way to the end.

11. Aristide's Day

Exhausted by the emotions of the tragic evening Aristide fell asleep in an armchair when he got back to the house the next morning. He did not wake up until the valet brought him the mail and morning newspapers. The blue slip of a telegram caught his attention. It was sent from Le Havre and signed by his architect:

Monsieur, I've read about the disaster in all the local newspapers. Bad news. The worst! The insurance contracts that you hired me to negotiate have not yet been signed, which means the Company probably won't accept them. Nevertheless, I will deal with it when I get back to Paris. I'm deeply sorry for the bad luck that's hit me as well as you. M.S.

More than the fire and after the Phoenician castle, this news marked the ruin of the young doctor. He remained, however, relatively calm, perhaps even cold. He opened the newspapers and quickly skimmed through them. Most of them reported the disaster, but it was "last minute" and with no details. They only expressed their hope that the Art in Cordat's house had escaped the fire, since it had been put on the ground floor; but it was too soon to go into detail about the event.

Aristide was not overly surprised by a natural restraint under such circumstances. Moreover, he did not have much time to dwell on things because by the time he had finished a quick review of the first news, the bell started ringing over and over again, which warned him that he was already prey for the journalists.

He saw two of them who came carrying an extra edition of the Matinée, 3rd edition, with headlines across the front page: FIRE AT L'ETOILE. He scanned the story that they showed him, but found nothing unusual except the news of the deaths resulting from the disaster and the temporary address where Doctor Cordat and his house staff had taken refuge. With this he quickly bid farewell to the two journalists telling them that he was too tired to be of any use to them and he refused to see anyone else for the same reason.

It was good to play it safe. For one or two hours the bell was rung constantly by messengers and men eager for information, but they had to make do with the house staff to get any new details about the news of the day. Aristide was exhausted by the events of the day before and tired of repeating the main circumstances surrounding the drama, so he obeyed his basic instincts and declined any new interviews or even to talk about his troubles, but it wasn't out of any real hostility toward the press agents. "After all, they're just doing their job and they have to do it in good conscience," he said if he was asked his personal opinion. But for now it was the least of his worries. He was only thinking about avoiding any extra, useless chores.

He soon learned at his own expense how rash and dangerous such an attitude was. Since the impact of his debut the representatives of "the third power," that is the press, had got used to considering him a public figure and a natural source of information. They were surprised and disappointed to find themselves promptly snubbed when they offered to become the kind editors of the "eminently Parisian" event. And by a kind of tacit agreement they were offering the very version that the interested party could hope for. So, Messieurs the journalists resented his resistance, which was right away translated into open hostility: in short, a natural hostility toward him who knew the ins and outs of the affair and refused to make their job easier by giving them ready-made articles. And by a logical turn they went right away to those who could give them some information, true or false. The professional reviews reproduced the stormy debate at the Academy of Medicine concerning the operations at the Cordat house. The reporters who knew their job did not take long to follow this lead. Rejected at 9 a.m. by Doctor Cordat, at 11 they were at Velpeau Hospital with Professor Bordier and they only had to take out their notebooks and copy down what was said because the entire staff, from the big boss and the physicians down to the lowliest intern were talking about nothing but the fire on Avenue du Bois, its supposed causes, its suspicious preliminaries and its probable results.

Professor Bordier was still fuming from his recent quarrel over the marvelous operations attributed to Doctor Cordat and did not hesitate to blame the events of the night before, about which he knew very little, on the most despicable and criminal motives. In his view the fire was plotted by the principal party because of the impossible situation he *must have* found himself in after spending so much money on his absurd luxuries. In the disaster he tried to hide the fact that he was going to end up in financial and surgical bankruptcy. The so-called "experiments" of the young Cordat were nothing but a myth, a scam, a trap set up for the naïve public; a shameful publicity stunt that its author finally couldn't deal with. He was overwhelmed by all kinds of responsibilities. When he saw that things were getting out of hand and he could not justify his crazy claims, he decided to drown everything in a torrent of purifying water—from the firemen. As for the murder of the unfortunate prosector of the Ecole Pratique, followed so soon after by the execution of Baron Tasimoura and the two unknown people now lying in the Morgue, all of this was highly suspicious and should be investigated immediately. It would be too soon to get ahead of the police by expressing a definite opinion before knowing the details of the affair and the conclusion of the forensic experts. But at first sight you had to think that it all smelled fishy and nothing good could come of it.

"Whoever lives will see!" the professor said like a seer while sawing the femur of an unlucky cart driver who had his thigh crushed under a 4000 pound stone. "While waiting, gentlemen, let's mind our own business, as they say. And let me repeat that it's better to stick to good old-fashioned surgery and perform normal, clumsy amputations when they are called for than to run such tragic, suspicious and dangerous risks."

These memorable words were spoken at 11:45 a.m. They were reported right away by young Blaisot, a part-time reporter for the *Telegraph*, the same one who bragged that he never had problems finishing a sentence once he had begun it (for better or worse) because "the main point was not to dazzle the reader by the purity of a faultless style, but to fill him up with information and a wealth of details." Whether such details were printed in Occitan or in French did not matter to this imaginary reader or to Blaisot. And he wasted no time on stupid corrections. He caught a cab and doubled the tip. At 12:15 on Rue Croissant his article was rolling off on the endless paper sacrificed to the wet kisses of the press. Twenty minutes later it was flying onto Boulevard Montmartre and booming out of the lips or two or three dozen paperboys. "Get the *Telegraph*! Latest news! Professor Bordier's opinion on the mystery of Avenue du Bois!"

There was already a "mystery" rising like fresh bread. At around 2 when Aristide Cordat arrived at the Palais de Justice to answer the telegram of the investigating judge Collineau, he bought a copy of the memorable opinion interpreted by young Blaisot and glanced at it as he went up the stairs to the Cour de Mai. This quick look was enough to give him a foretaste of what to expect. Maybe it was the scaffold! You never know... Anyway, it was the vicious hiss and filthy breath of slander. Now it was not just a matter of clearing up the tragic situation created by the successive deaths of Joel Le Berquin, Spiridon, Pia Baselli and her father, it was a matter of exonerating the honesty of the one who had presented to the world the paradox of the ant operations in an exclusive and terribly sensational experiment.

"There is no longer a question of holding back anything that has to do with the innovation," he told himself when he got to the top of the stairs. "Put everything before the judge and before the public, that's what counts! The rest doesn't matter."

But to clear up such a complicated affair was not as easy as Aristide imagined. At first Judge Collineau did not know anything about it. He had just been transferred from a subprefecture court and he knew nothing about science. He was a hard working, upright man who sincerely sought the truth in the cases given to him, but he was bitter in his searching since in his eyes everything was a problem of either normal or pathological physiology. Aristide explained things very clearly, just as he had done with the Public Prosecutor, but it was easy to see that he was wasting his time. He was speaking a foreign language to a man who only cared about the legal aspects of his investigation. He became utterly exhausted by the effort he made to begin again, for the third or fourth time in 24 hours, the analysis of the prickly drama where he stood center stage. When he left the judge's office at around 6 p.m., he did not want to do anything but be alone and hear nothing about the tedious investigation. He was way out of it.

The army of informants was notified of his presence at the Palais and was waiting for him in the hallway and on the stairs. When he came out there was a veritable riot of reporters who pushed and shoved one another to get the details of the interview. He brushed them rudely aside, humble but firm, telling them that he had told the judge everything he knew about the matter under investigation. He said that his statement no longer belonged to him and, besides, he was too tired to tell the story over again. Then he got free, went down the stairs, jumped in a carriage and ordered the driver to take him to Bois de Boulogne.

And there is no need to say that he was followed right away, kept in sight of two or three of his torturers who also took number cabs to escort him.

Aristide was infuriated by their perseverance and when he got to l'Etoile he gave up the idea of going for a walk and went back home on foot, giving orders to keep everyone out.

But he could not keep out the mail, which flooded his address with letters and telegrams. One of the telegrams came from Professor Falcimaigne: "Have a casual dinner with us if you have the time. Important things to tell you."

Aristide thought that he could do worse than answer the call. He got dressed after having a look at the evening papers, which were literally crammed with pretty far-fetched details about the day's events and then he left in his car.

The professor had not come back yet. His daughter, Gertrude, was alone with her mother and said that he would not be long and was very anxious to talk with Doctor Cordat. He had mentioned his desire to see him several times during the day and sent a trusted employee to tell him.

While she was talking the professor came in.

"Finally, my dear friend, here you are!" he shook his former student's hand warmly. "I've been looking for you since this morning and I just went by your house again to get some news. I was eager to see you and tell you what happened. They're talking about nothing but you in Paris. Did you get any details about the Ecole Pratique?"

"No, in fact. I went to the Palais where I spent a not very amusing day in an interview with the judge and his clerk. I told him everything I know and I hope it's over with for now. As far as the Ecole Pratique is concerned, I know nothing about it."

"Well, here's what happened. The experts assigned by the prosecution service went with the Chief of Police to take away Le Berquin's remains. They took all the containers in the laboratory to transport them to the Morgue under the watch of a police officer. And along with the containers they took a few of the "elastic" prosthetics of Ozoud, which were apparently used to disguise or mask the real identity of Tasimoura. At least, that was what the experts thought, which slipped out to me inadvertently. Do you know anything about this?"

"The experts' opinions are perfectly well-founded!" Doctor Cordat answered right away, smiling for the first time in 48 hours. "Do they think they have found something important?"

"In fact, they do," the professor replied, not so casually. "They were wondering why Tasimoura, if he really was ambushed and trapped in the Ecole Pratique, was dressed up in such a costume with prosthetics."

"Really? The experts have run up against this problem? Well, that's reassuring and gives a good idea of their competence!" Aristide laughed out loud. "My dear teacher, I don't doubt for a minute that in a moment of hesitation you put your finger on the simple solution to this nerve-racking problem. Tasimoura was stripped of these prosthetics one by one that were meant to mask what his body was missing. He wore them all the time. He had them on during the operations you witnessed at my house. He wouldn't show himself in public for anything in the world without the borrowed radiance of this armor, which was supplied, as you said, by Ozoud, who will bear witness to the fact. And it's exactly because he was never separated from them that he was wearing them when he was detoured on Rue Monsieur le Prince by that poor wretch Le Berquin. I'll also tell you that in my personal opinion it was to verify the nature of this get-up that the prosector thought of trapping Tasimoura and knocking him out. The sequence of events apparently led him to decide to kill him when he first only wanted to strip him of his secrets."

"That is very probable!" the professor mumbled thoughtfully and obviously preoccupied. "Although now this revelation seems to be the crux of the matter. The experts think very differently about it!"

"What do they think?" Aristide was completely surprised.

"It'd be pretty hard for me to say. But the mysterious air about them seemed pretty menacing. I wouldn't be surprised if they ended up with something huge—a plot devised against Le Berquin with aggravating circumstances of the prosthetics and mask in place of a false beard."

"You really think they're stupider than nature? As low as my opinion is of licensed experts, I wouldn't dare to go so far as think them capable of such a thing."

"You're wrong, my dear friend. Human stupidity and meanness always go farther than you would think. And I seriously fear that they are going to give us a brilliant example before too long. You don't seem to have a very good idea of the anger and jealousy that your operations stirred up in the profession. Anger knows no bounds. It has already affected those whom you chose to witness your famous experiment. I wouldn't be at all surprised if it ends up in some monstrous accusation."

"And what accusation would that be?"

"How would I know? They'll say that the whole thing is a conspiracy! That everything is phony and false like your assistant's appearance. That Le Berquin, your schoolmate and personal friend, was onto the plot. That he was forced by his conscience to reveal it. That it was necessary to get rid of this dangerous witness at any price. That it was Tasimoura's job to do away with him. Won't they say that, dear boy? They've already insinuated, I'm sure, even though no one has told me so directly, that you made Tasimoura disappear after he killed Le Berquin and that the fire in your house was necessary as the crowning solution to an inevitable financial and scientific defeat."

"It's not possible! It's already gone that far?" Aristide cried out. "I can't believe it. In any case," he clenched his fists, "we'll find out who's saying this, I swear! You can't just insinuate such slanderous remarks; you have to prove it! And I'll challenge all of these so-called experts and the stupid troublemakers hiding behind them. I've already decided that it would be better to speak frankly about everything concerning Tasimoura, Le Berquin and myself; and I did so yesterday to the Public Prosecutor and the Chief of Police before the fire. I did so again today with the investigating judge and his clerk of the court. I will do it again, if necessary, either in a court of law or anywhere else!"

"Dear boy, trust in my instinct and affection: you have to go even farther than that to destroy all this vileness. It's not enough just to explain what happened last night and bring it out in the open...*above all else you have to reproduce in my clinic or somewhere else what you did in front of us in your laboratory.* Two or three decisive, brilliant operations so that no one can have any doubt or suspicion about the reality of the experiments."

Professor Falcimaigne had barely pronounced these words when he saw Aristide's body break down, so to speak, and become deadly pale.

"My dear teacher, that's precisely what I cannot do! I can't reproduce the experiment I did in front of you because Tasimoura kept the secret of the liquids we used...and the fire destroyed everything. And by the way, if there was any need to prove my total innocence in the disaster, I think that that should be proof enough, not considering the fact that the fire ruined me in every way because the insurance contract was not yet signed!"

"There's always something to be gained from a great misfortune and maybe you should be thankful for it!" the professor answered philosophically. "But still, couldn't you recreate Tasimoura's formulae? I'm sure you have some clues about it to help you."

"I have clues, of course. In particular the orders I signed following Tasimoura's instructions so he could get the chemicals he needed. These orders can easily be found again at the stores he went to, but even finding them again, I have only a vague idea to figure out the secret that I know nothing about, not to mention the skill that Tasimoura always refused to teach me."

"Damn! Damn! Why was he so secretive?"

"I always thought it had something to do with tradition, maybe hieratic. He was the depository of a secret that was probably his source of power. See, he was the unrivaled leader of his species, passed on from father to son, just like he was the highest representative of it because of his strength, size and intelligence. He obviously considered himself invested with a duty that was both sacred and sovereign, by virtue of the enduring right that he held over these traditions through a continual transmission since the time of the Phoenicians or Chaldeans. I imagine that he was initiated in the respect for these secret traditions at a very young age. At least that's the theory that I came up with after many clues, especially because it was always impossible for me to get the slightest information about this out of him. And the unfortunate Le Berquin probably ran up against the same savage silence. I'm sure that's what prompted his unspeakable attack. He paid for it with his life. As for me, I was waiting for the right time, for a chance, an opportunity or a gradual solution to the problem and quite simply that's why I didn't publish the secret, which I didn't even have yet."

"All this is perfectly logical and is no problem for someone of good faith. But we're not dealing with people of good faith here, my dear friend! And that's why you have to retrace your experiments or we'll be sunk for good in the affair!"

"I feel the same way! And that's why I'm going to stop at nothing to accomplish it. But will I be able to retrace the thread that was so quickly cut from my hands? I want to with all my heart, dear teacher, but I shouldn't hope for too much."

The dinner bell interrupted this confidential meeting, but it was only a short break. Professor Falcimaigne was used to speaking freely about his research in front of his wife and daughter. He did not believe it was necessary to hide from them what he was so rightly busy with, so he started talking again with Aristide at the table.

"You have to hurry up your investigation of the chemists," he said out of the blue. "Find your orders tomorrow and then hammer away at it and reconstruct your elixirs as best you can. If you only find a partial or even insignificant result, it will be better than nothing. Believe me, hurry up, there's no time to lose. Give these jackals a bone to chew on!"

12. Brotherly Comments

The next day's newspapers brought to the public a summary of the experts' conclusions which had just been completed at the Morgue and obviously communicated to the agents of information by the Public Prosecutor's Department. The very lengthy paper can be summed up as follows:

"It follows from these verifications that there seems to be no immediate connection among the circumstances surrounding the death of Joel Le Berquin, prosector of the School of Medicine, on the one hand and those of Spiridon Tasimoura, Antonio Baselli and Pia Baselli on the other.

"Concerning Joel Le Berquin, his death was obviously preceded by the use of anesthesia, particularly a strong agent whose traces and odor were discovered in a flask on a shelf of chemical products in the laboratory. The flask was empty, but had the address of Janiot, a first rate pharmacist at Pilon d'Or, 51bis Rue Saint Denis, Paris. The death appears to have been caused by the methodical extraction of the main organs—lungs, heart, liver and intestines—from the chest and abdomen after a 20 inch incision was made down the median line. The organs were placed on the dissection table along with the eyes and brain after they were taken out. The very clean removal of these different organs proves that the perpetrator of the mutilation had some professional skill.

"Concerning Spiridon Tasimoura, so named, the experts are being very cautious since they cannot determine his age, even approximately, or the species of animal he belongs to. For this a supplementary examination by authorized entomologists from the Museum of Natural History could be useful. For the time being, considering the outward appearance of the subject, the undersigned experts figure that it must be classed among the most unusual and extraordinary specimens of abnormal beings that they have ever examined or even seen mentioned in the annals of forensic medicine. It's a kind of monster whose main features resemble a colossal insect, in particular a giant ant—a typical head with two pairs of faceted eyes, powerful mandibles, a narrow thorax and thick abdomen surrounded by a horny carapace, two jointed forelimbs for arms and two atrophied legs for feet, whose stumps and tendrils are clearly recognizable on the sides of the thoracic cage. In the presence of such a clear case of animal aberration the undersigned experts do not feel especially qualified for a dissection that could be more usefully performed by professional entomologists. They willfully limit themselves to the examination of the circumstances surrounding the cause of the death and have noted:

1. The clear sign of burns on the lower limbs caused by a corrosive liquid that left red marks on the horny skin of these limbs;

2. On one of the left lateral eyes, a wound made by a piercing instrument, presumably a knife with a triangular blade, which split the faceted cornea and penetrated into the brain, evidenced by the hernia of this organ in the orbit. As a secondary but still notable circumstance of the examination that the experts performed, it's worthwhile noting that in the search of the laboratory of the deceased prosector they found two artificial devices, called prosthetics and stamped by Ozoud. Apparently they were made to be used as lower limbs for the so-called Spiridon Tasimoura. The head of the aforemen-

tioned Ozoud Company was immediately summoned before us and right away acknowledged that these artificial coverings came from his workshop at the request and following the instructions of Doctor Cordat for Spiridon Tasimoura to use. He added that he supplied these devices on demand and sent them on October 3 to Doctor Cordat at the train station in Marseille.

3. Concerning Antonio Baselli, tuna fisherman, former petty officer third class of the Italian navy, originally from Sardinia, 55 years old, found dead at the foot of the main staircase at the Cordat residence a short time after the fire of said residence and taken away by the firemen on duty. His death appears to have been caused by a headfirst, 100-foot fall onto the marble floor. The fall broke his spine and crushed his skull, causing a loss of cerebral matter.

"4. Concerning Pia Baselli, daughter of above named, also originally from Sardinia, around 22 years old, death caused by a stiletto with a triangular blade that she stabbed into her precordial region in the presence of the Chief of Police and several firemen on the discovery of the dead body of Spiridon Tasimoura among the ruins of the fire. Pia Baselli regularly carried this stiletto on her person. She stabbed herself with her right hand. The weapon pierced the heart without tearing its cavities, which explains why she did not die for 10 to 12 minutes afterward, enough time to bring her down to the lawn in the yard.

"Conclusion:

1. Joel Le Berquin, prosector of the School of Medicine, died in a state of anaesthetized unconsciousness, of the removal of his vital organs from his chest, abdomen and skull with the use of a scalpel and handsaw belonging to himself, which were found on the dissection

table where his remains were lying when the authorities arrived.

2. Spiridon Tasimoura, so named, died of a wound inflicted by a triangular, piercing weapon (probably Pia Baselli's stiletto) that penetrated the encephalon through the lateral left eye creating a deep wound with a hernia of the organ in the orbit. Prior violence had been inflicted on his skull with a blunt instrument (probably a hammer or an iron bar).

3. Antonio Baselli died after a headfirst, 100-foot fall onto the marble floor. The fall caused a fractured skull and loss of cerebral matter.

"4. Pia Baselli killed herself in the presence of several witnesses by piercing her heart with a Sardinian stiletto, which she usually carried around with her. With regard to this, the placement and direction of the wound corresponds to the hypothesis of suicide witnessed by the above named.

"Signed,

"Doctor Veret and Doctor Anthrax."

As if there were need of a decisive commentary on this official publication, which agreed with Professor Falcimaigne's warning about the danger of the situation, the "Surgical Gazette" published an ominous note the next day. The gloss was not signed, but from the first glance Aristide Cordat recognized the style and manner of Professor Bordier. The article not only reproduced in veiled terms all the malicious gossip that was spreading around town, but it treated them as if they were given facts. And the dramatic title was "The Tragedy in Bois de Boulogne":

"The experts' report filed after the examination of the victims of the carnage at the Ecole Pratique that reached its conclusion on Avenue du Bois, was released to the press at the same time as it arrived at the Public Prosector's Department. Since it is a document that is going to be the foundation of an open criminal investigation of the tragedy, the report contains only a statement of the forensic results. It does not deal with the questions that necessarily arise about the preparation and development of the tragedy or its direct or indirect perpetrators: it gives no opinion on the subject. It simply says: here is what we saw on the funeral slabs in the Morgue; here are the material facts we could get from the four corpses presented for our examination; here is the factual foundation that we offer to the judgment and discussion of learned men while waiting for the matter to be handed over to the verdict of 12 citizens responsible for pronouncing judgment without hatred or fear on the penal aspects of this dreadful drama.

"This foundation is as follows. A young, most highly respected surgeon, two-time prizewinner of the hospitals of Paris, assigned to the highest post the Faculty of Medicine can give to its members and future professors, was found dead on the battlefield, which was his dissection table in the laboratory that he ran at the Ecole Pratique. He was not just purely and simply dead as so often happened to his predecessors and will undoubtedly happen to more than one of his successors following that fatal sting, that is the anatomical sting—but he was cut open, ripped open and disemboweled with his eyes, liver, heart, lungs and finally his nerve center torn out by a hand as skilled as it was criminal. You could say that it left an authentic signature on its abominable work by the professional skill it displayed.

"To leave nothing out of the picture, the dutiful hero, the outright victim of devotion to science was knocked out with chloroform before he was torn to pieces in a sacrilegious use of the noblest conquest of modern surgery. He was tied down to his table with his own straps. He was covered with a sheet belonging to the hospital. And through clumsy carelessness, not to say, above all else, strangely suspicious (and apparently meant to lead the prosecution on a false trail), the perpetrator of this monstrous butchery left behind two prosthetic devices that were custom-made for one of his assistants by a well known specialist and that would, at first sight, surely implicate this helper in the terrible crime.

"Of course this ally had to disappear before he could explain his role, which is what happened! Only a few hours after the police were led, as if by the hand, to the site of the massacre, at the very moment when the apparent whistleblower was meeting with the Public Prosecutor in person to give him his version of the story, cleverly worked out beforehand, at this very moment the man with the prosthetics disappeared in a fire that they are now blaming on him, just like everything else.

"We call him *the man*. It seems that he was not even this! The experts' report says in no uncertain terms that he must be classed in the category of insects. Maybe that's going a little far. That's the version of some entomologists who were authorized to give their opinion. So this insect, or so-called insect, who is now charged with the crimes and earlier was introduced under a false title and dressed up from head to foot, cannot explain himself before a court or anywhere else because he is dead, just in time! Too much in time, for sure! It is true that he was mute, or so they imagine. The fact remains that his testimony could have been dangerous in more than one way, seeing that he disappeared for it!

"He would have been called to give, either in writing or hand signals, explanations about certain difficult surgical operations that have recently made a lot more fuss than they deserve, undoubtedly. And it is apparently in this direction that we should search for the key to the mystery, if there still is a mystery!

"The operations had been rigged, just like the anatomy of the famous "Baron" who suddenly became an ant again! They will no doubt find a few more prosthetics—cardboard lungs and an aneurysm just for a laugh. That's how it will be or never again say like the storyteller of old did about the Mountain in labor: *Nascitur ridiculus mus...*[7] and less than a rat, an insect! Oh, how the passion for publicity can drive our hustling contemporaries to such wretched schemes! It leads them first into strange partnerships and later to appalling crimes. In the development of this drama we are going to follow step by step the sad results of this sickness that belongs to the young people of this century and that in the present case has already claimed four victims, one of whom will always be missed and the other three unknown but still worthy of our pity. Their roles will come out little by little. We will find out where the "Baron" came from and what the Sardinian fisherman who spilled his brains on the marble had to do with the tragedy, along with his daughter who wielded the knife with so much skill. The rest will fall upon the wretched worker of a monstrous surgical farce that was obviously intended to cover up a simple scam and that will ultimately bring down all those who willingly helped this crook

---

[7] The mountain labored and gave birth to a ridiculous mouse (Horace).

who cheated his sponsors and the upholders of public opinion."

On reading this venomous prose, Aristide rushed off to Professor Falcimaigne's house to ask for his advice. Should he take the newspaper to court and demand that they justify this slander? Or should he rather start the process by claiming latent defamation of character at the hospital or at the School of Medicine and demand a public apology that would force the author to clear up Aristide's blackened name? He got there boiling with rage and to his bitter disappointment right away learned from Mademoiselle and Madame Falcimaigne that when the professor left for his morning rounds at the hospital he had to take a train to Limoges for a serious, emergency operation.

Aristide was too angry to stay calm and could not hold back his fits of rage in front of the two women whom he knew were on his side. In a nutshell he told them the cause of his anger and worry. He had come to his revered teacher to look for a word of encouragement and comfort. In fact, he needed honest and objective advice in the face of such terrible accusations. He had to answer his slanderers and answer them fast, no matter what the consequences. That's what he had come to see the professor about. If needed he would catch the first train to meet up with him, so he asked the ladies for the address where he could send a telegram to set up a meeting at a station on the way.

Madame Falcimaigne and her daughter volunteered to send the telegram that Doctor Cordat thought was indispensable. But wouldn't it be better to wait until evening for the professor or until first thing in the morning at the Quai d'Orsay station? To arrange the meeting he only had to notify his teacher and find out from him the exact time of his return. Aristide easily surrendered to such a sensible proposition. The message was written and sent right then.

When this was done, Aristide felt calmer and went into detail about his ordeal. He had searched the pharmacies, found some of the orders he had written at Spiridon's request and others that the Baron had written himself. But even when he remembered some of the specifics, it unfortunately did not give him any information about the preparation of the elixirs used by his collaborator. And there was not a drop of them left! The fire consumed everything. Approximations, trials and errors were still possible and that is what Aristide was going to do as soon as he found a laboratory. But that would take time! And he had to act right away, right now, to respond to the vile plot organized against him and his dear teacher!

As he was talking, Gertrude was staring at him with trembling lips and when this mighty sadness exploded out of him, she suddenly said, "A laboratory? But don't you have the one you set up for Baron Tasimoura in your current residence? A Russian family whom we sent to the place last week to ask to rent your former apartment wasn't able to get it *because you still had two months paid in advance*. The landlord was going to ask you to arrange it so they could move in, but the family changed their minds and found something on Champs Elysées."

"That's true!" Aristide jumped to his feet, clutching the hope that suddenly appeared before him. "I paid for the apartments until April and since I've been back I've never thought of opening the three rooms that belonged to Tasimoura above my office. If there's any chance that they've stayed intact, my dear friend, you cannot know what an invaluable service you have just done for me by this lucky reminder. But I'll wait until I've made sure. Excuse me, ladies, I'll see you tonight. I'll see you soon!"

He dashed off and without even realizing that he had forgotten his hat he ran straight down Avenue Hoche.

"The laboratory? The Baron's apartment?" he asked as he burst into the building's office, where he had hardly ever entered before. "What happened to the three rooms that the Baron used when we were living here together?"

"Monsieur Doctor, I don't think that they've disappeared," said the very elegant young lady watching over the fate of the register under her blond hair. And she gave him the calmest smile in the world, "They're still on the third floor and at your disposal. I'll call for the valet."

She pressed a button that rang a bell on the upper floors, but before the valet had time to respond, Aristide rushed over to the numbered board where a dozen keys were hanging.

"It was number 9, if I'm not mistaken," he said nervously as he took the key.

"It was and still is 9," the young lady answered.

"It's vacant, isn't it?"

"Of course, Doctor, unless you decided to rent it. We even thought of asking you recently if we could give it to a Russian lady who was referred here by Professor Falcimaigne, but you'd paid for the apartment until April so we didn't follow up on the idea."

The young lady continued her clever, little explanation, but Aristide was not listening. With the blessed key in hand he bounded up the stairs three at a time. When he got to the third floor, he opened up the door of room 9 with a trembling hand and went straight through the sitting room and the bedroom and barged into the waiting room, which was an old kitchen where daylight entered from the courtyard, and finally he was in...Spiridon's laboratory. It was exactly the same as the memorable day when the giant ant had left to go to Avenue du Bois!

Nothing was missing. Everything was where he had left it: the basin of mercury set up in an old sandstone fountain, the reverbatory furnace still half-full of wood coal, the glass balls, test tubes, cupules, reagent glasses and above all... Oh! Joy! Oh! Exhilaration beyond compare! On the long, white shelves a bunch of corked bottles were lined up. The doctor recognized them at first sight, and later by smell and taste: the mysterious elixirs prepared by Spiridon that he had been desperate to recreate!

With infinite precaution and bitter joy the young doctor went through the inventory, hardly believing the unexpected luck that fell upon him by the simple suggestion of Gertrude. And now he was standing before the radiant horizon that this discovery opened up! Ah! How many of these piled up, dusty bottles that looked so commonplace would suddenly change the face of things! What a brilliant victory and total revenge they would bring against those who vilified him so cruelly! It was a sure and immediate triumph. It was Aristide's honor that these flasks contained within their thin walls. He touched them with a trembling hand, but did not yet dare to open them. And yet he clearly saw, like tangible evidence, what a bottomless pit had opened up beneath him for a few hours of unforgettable anxiety without these glass containers and what hidden power was sleeping within their precious walls.

From now on he would protect these irrefutable proofs of an uncheckered past and guarantees of a glorious future. Above all, he had to keep them out of reach...

Aristide slipped out of the poor giant ant's apartment. Locked the door behind him and went to his room to get some towels and a big wooden rack that he put the precious bottles in with the utmost care. When he came back safely from his expedition, he put the rack in the armoire next to the head of his bed and now that he was reassured about the future he wanted to give Gertrude the thanks she deserved.

On the way he passed by a flower shop and bought a bouquet of violets.

13. Complications

When Aristide rang the bell at Professor Falcimaigne's house, he was not the same man who had been there three hours earlier in the height of despair and bitterness. Gertrude and her mother were delighted to learn that the suggestion proved so quickly and decisively successful. They accepted the young doctor's thanks with sincere joy and wanted to tell the great news to the professor without delay. They wrote a second telegram:

No use changing plans. Vital bottles found in Tasimoura's first lab at Gertrude's suggestion. Everyone happy. Georges will wait at the station unless heard otherwise.

After sending the note they continued to celebrate and congratulate until Aristide decided to leave and return home with the evening newspapers. When he opened them he saw that the venomous article from the *Surgical Gazette* had been eagerly copied, which showed both its special contents and a hidden agreement among the informers to highlight whatever might be detrimental to the one who left them out in the cold. A few went so far as to declare in no uncertain terms that with the emotions raised by the experts' report and the general outcry of competent men, the Prosecution had to hand over the sinister affair to the court to be argued and settled in public.

A few hours earlier Aristide Cordat would have received this news quite differently. Now he took it lightheartedly, like a Roman conqueror once took the usual outrage of the stooges who represented the slaves defeated in his retinue.

When he got home he found a letter from the Secretary of the Anthropological Society on his desk.

"Dear Doctor and honored colleague," wrote the passionate collector of skulls and brains, "I don't know if you are familiar with Baron Tasimoura's testament during his memorable visit to the Dupuytren Museum, signed in the presence of myself and the late prosector of the School of Medicine, Doctor Le Berquin, that he left in my hands. Keeping with a venerable custom that renders notable service to science and that promises so much more, Baron Tasimoura by his testament bequeathed to the Mutual Autopsy Society, an adjunct of the Anthropological Society, the right to claim his mortal remains, especially his brain, for the direct examination by his colleagues who are specially devoted to studies of this kind and, as the case may be, to keep it in the collection that is already so rich. During the too brief period that I was in relation with Baron Tasimoura, I was keenly struck by his extraordinary physiognomy. What I read in the report of the two experts assigned by the court for the autopsy, which was needed in the sudden, premature death of Baron Tasimoura, has only made me firmer in the belief that in this case a detailed study would be of special interest to supply essential information on the physiology of his brain! Moreover, from the beginning I have taken quick measures to make sure that the legal examination be limited to the strict necessities by counting on the rights of science. Honored colleague, you certainly saw in the experts' report that they stated that they were not competent, or not enough, and wisely limited themselves to noting the exterior appearance of the wound and they offered the more detailed examination to the best entomologists in the field, notably the professors at the Museum of Natural History.

I can certainly imagine that this attitude was motivated by the measures I took, but nothing can keep me from saying that such a situation would be as opposed to the rights of the Mutual Autopsy Society as it would be to the interests of biological science. The representatives of the Prosecution have, in fact, arranged to study the matter from the legal point of view. For now they have fulfilled their duty without touching the brain and they have left it intact, whereby they were certainly wise since they recognized their incompetence. But it is not up to them to deal with what belongs, without question, by a signed testament, to the above-named Society. So, I have recourse to you, Doctor and honored colleague, to know if you, as a personal friend, host and executor of the will of the late Baron Tasimoura, would be willing to join us in claiming what rightfully belongs to us, to protect our interests and let us alone carry out the examination that the deceased freely chose us to do by a formal testament.

"I look forward to hearing from you soon. Yours sincerely. Signed. Doctor Pierre Micromegas."

The content of the letter left Aristide pretty confused both because it raised a very sticky legal point and because it just reminded him, inadvertently, that for three whole days since the incidents of the terrible affair, he had not bothered to ask about what became of the victims of the fire.

He ended up thinking that it would be best if he went to the Morgue. If he left now he would arrive just before they closed the doors.

The official at the sinister asylum gave a warm welcome to the famous visitor presenting his card. He met him on the steps, took him right away to the cold room and showed him the dead stretched out side by side on the marble slabs slanted toward the two-way mirrors that the public can walk by all day long.

Aristide was deeply moved when he saw Pia lying near her father and on another slab Spiridon was covered with a sheet and his forehead was wrapped in a bandage. He found out that the remains of Joel Le Berquin had been claimed by his family immediately after the examination and had already left for his birthplace near Chartres. A bitter cold from the blocks of ice hidden under the exhibition tables gripped the room. The young doctor felt it and could not keep from shivering. The official did not have to repeat his invitation to go to his office to warm up by the stove.

"What's the process to get authorization to bury the victims?" he asked.

"In general, the authorization is only given to immediate family," the city official answered. "Anyway, it has to be obtained from the Prefect of Police, who is the only one who can give it."

"Do you think that I can see him now if I went to Boulevard du Palais?"

"Unlikely. He usually only sees people in the morning, but you can certainly find a secretary or an assistant in his office to give you some precise information or at least to take your request, if you intend to go ahead with the funerals. I'm sure Headquarters received the experts' conclusions this morning that would authorize the removal of the two Italians, father and daughter... As for the other, they're calling it a monster, a kind of gigantic insect, as you probably know, Doctor, and the experts have referred it to a second opinion by the professors at the Museum of Natural History. But they haven't said whether they'll take care of it. And besides, today a bailiff presented me with a protest by the Anthropological

Society trying to get Baron Tasimoura's remains granted to them instead of anyone else, even for the examination that they claim belongs to them through some testament they have."

"And who makes the decision about this?"

"It depends. The Prefect of Police might be able to do it if he really thinks it's an animal or he can leave it to the Prosecution if he has any doubt about it."

"All in all it's the Prefect who has control over the matter, isn't it?"

"Like in everything that affects the short-term tenants that we are here," the Morgue official said with a kind of gruesome laugh.

"Thank you, Monsieur, and I'm going to go right away to see if I can meet with the Prefect, in spite of how late it is."

Aristide got up and said goodbye to the city official, who wasted no time locking the doors and windows of the institution behind him.

The automobile reached Police Headquarters within three minutes. Following the friendly directions given by a guardian of the peace on duty at the foot of the stairs, Doctor Cordat went up to the Prefect's office and presented his card. An assistant came to tell him that the Prefect would see him in spite of the unusual time "because he was just about to call him to ask him to come urgently…"

Everything was explained when the visitor went in.

"I was just going to ask you to come to see me," the Prefect said," because things don't seem to be going as well as expected at the Prosecution. It looks like there's an incredible plot against you that's taking over everything. They're flooded with anonymous letters! People are accusing you of setting fire to your house after first killing the prosector and then your assistant, Baron Tasimoura, and finally the Italian visitors who came to your house that very day. They're saying that your surgical operations were nothing but a hoax; that you were backed into a corner by the enormous cost of your princely set-up; that you didn't know how to get out of the jam and the crimes supplied the means. I don't have to tell you that all this hue and cry is listened to with reservations. It was a good thing that you got the Chief of Police, the Public Prosecutor and myself to trust you completely by the honesty of the steps you undertook with such an unusual perseverance at the very time when the fire broke out and before the tragic events that caused all this to happen. But it doesn't look like the investigating judge or the experts share the same opinion as the Public Prosecutor and me. They think the case is not very clear and the charges weighing against you are maybe not terribly serious, but at least they're not insignificant. Plus, you can't deny that you've had what they call "bad press." Not only are both the morning and evening newspapers printing these things against you, which does not bode well for you, but the medical press is laying into you tooth and nail. They even brought me an article this afternoon by a Professor at the School of Medicine that accuses you, without naming you, in the most dangerous way. In brief, you're being attacked on every side and you should understand that such unanimity in the suspicions or in the gossip can't go unnoticed by the legal authorities. The Public Prosecutor wants to see me about this and has made it clear that in your interest and in the interest of justice, he might soon be forced to ask you to justify yourself publicly, like you did in your private office."

The Prefect stopped there. He hesitated to continue and his hesitation was like a ray of hope for Aristide.

"Do you mean that they're thinking of filing charges against me?" he suddenly cried out and jumped to his feet. "Monsieur Prefect, I advise against this because the magistrate who would take on such a responsibility would be committing a great injustice and be setting himself up for a bitter disappointment! I swear my justification will be spectacular and will fall back on whoever accuses me, right there on the spot!"

"Are you sure of that? Have you got hold of irrefutable evidence?" the Prefect asked skeptically, as the police usually do.

"I have got hold of evidence that I would love to put before the public, so certain am I that it will humiliate everyone slandering me."

"If you have evidence like that, dear doctor, let me advise you to bring it out as soon as possible. There's not much time. And no one would be happier than me—I really mean that."

"What should I do? Ask to be arrested and face my accusers?"

"That would be useless since they're anonymous. They would shy away and things would be no better. Truthfully, I don't really know what to say," the Prefect looked thoughtful. "Let's see, are you a man of action? Can you burn your ships and jump in open water?"

"Yes, of course, if it takes me straight to my goal."

"Well, if you are sure of yourself, I mean if you really do have irrefutable proof of your total innocence, why not ask the Prosecution to bring you before the Court to present the proof that you claim to have?"

"That's an idea. And you won't be able to deny it, Monsieur Prefect," Aristide went over to the desk. "I'll write the letter right now in front of you and ask you to send it yourself to the Prosecution."

Saying this, Aristide grabbed a chair, sat in front of the Prefect and without a moment's hesitation he quickly wrote the following on an official sheet of paper that was lying on the desk:

"Monsieur Public Prosecutor,

"Unspeakable accusations have been leveled against me since the disaster and no one dares to take responsibility for them. They are insinuating that I am an impostor, a murderer and an arsonist. To allow these peddlers to come forth and to allow myself to prove their nonsense, I respectfully request you to bring me before the court at the earliest convenient date on the charges of murder and arson. I challenge those spreading these despicable accusations against me to bring them into court and for my part I promise to give irrefutable proof of my innocence in front of a jury.

"If you think it worthwhile, Monsieur, I will turn myself in while waiting for the proof. In any case, from this minute on I am voluntarily placing myself under the surveillance of the Prefect of Police, who is watching me write this letter on his desk in his office and will see to it that you receive the letter after copying it and sending it to the press. Yours Sincerely, Aristide Cordat."

"Very well," the Prefect said after reading it through. "But what do you mean by placing yourself under my surveillance?"

"I'm going to send away my car and take a carriage or walk. You can get two officers to follow me and keep me in sight day and night. If need be, they can sleep in my apartment. Or if you prefer, you can issue a warrant for my arrest and send me to the Conciergerie!"

"There's no point in that, Doctor. Personally, I believe in your total innocence. If the Prosecution wants to blunder around, that it's business, but I intend to wash my hands of the whole affair."

Doctor Cordat left the Headquarters, ordered his car to return home without him and, after waiting a few minutes on the sidewalk of Boulevard du Palais to make sure that he was under surveillance, he noticed that no one seemed to be following him. At first, he was surprised, then delighted. Obviously the Prefect was sincere when he said he believed in his total innocence. And this reminded him that, being carried away by his emotions, he had forgotten to mention the real purpose of his visit, which was to ask for authorization to give a decent burial to his friends. He was reluctant to go back again and beg the Prefect to deal with this secondary concern, so he decided to send a telegram. For this he found a post office nearby around the Commercial Court.

He sat at a table on the right, took some paper that was there for the public to use and wrote:

"Monsieur Prefect,

"The special purpose of my visit this evening, which our important conversation made me lose sight of, was to ask for authorization to take the remains of Pia Baselli and her father out of the Morgue and bury them. Also I would like to send the remains of Spiridon Tasimoura to the Mutual Autopsy Society in accordance with a signed testament that the secretary of this Society informed me of today. The purpose of this request is to proceed with an examination of the brain of the deceased in the presence of the members of the Society and other specialists, especially professors of natural history, who will be useful to the operation. I (as executor of the will and only friend here in Paris of the three victims whom you saw perish with your own eyes) respectfully request the necessary authorization to answer to their will and at the same time to the desires expressed by the experts with regard to Tasimoura, who is, indeed, as they saw, a gigantic ant.

"Yours Sincerely, Dr. Cordat, 225 Avenue Hoche."

After Aristide handed the telegram over the counter he took a walk down the quay toward Tuileries to go back to his temporary home, thinking about how he should react to whatever decision the court made about him. In any case, he had to go ahead with a public experiment of the inherent properties of the elixirs prepared by Spiridon, which were luckily found in his first Parisian apartment.

The experiment would take place in court if the Public Prosecutor and the Grand Jury agreed to it. Regardless of the Prosecution's decision, an experiment would take place in full light and be open to the public.

With his mind firmly made up, Aristide thought first about outlining a plan. Above all, he had to establish the unquestionable properties of the recovered medicine. Aristide would not hesitate to repeat his first statement, that he did not know the exact composition of the mode of preparation. Personally he had only experienced the wonderful effects: Firstly on himself when he was captured in the castle in Sardinia and dissected, for which he could still show the recent marks on his own arm; secondly on Spiridon whom he had shot twice, almost at point-blank range, and then brought on board his boat in a state of unconsciousness and with his head riddled with no.2 buckshot; thirdly, and lastly, on the three patients whom he had operated on in Paris with the help of Spiridon in the presence of a limited number of competent witnesses.

As a result of these facts and the bad opinions that they produced, two allotments were going to be made in public of the liquids left by Spiridon in his apartment on Avenue Hoche. One of these allotments would be delivered to three renowned chemists. These experts would perform a detailed analysis to determine the composition of the liquids under consideration and would publish the results for everyone to know in the *Journal of the Academy of Sciences*. From then on they would be in the public domain to serve all of humanity.

For his part, Doctor Cordat would reserve the right to show directly the properties of the other allotment of the liquids in question: 1st putting them to the proof in public on any living being chosen for the experiment and on any patient whose condition was considered hopeless and who would participate in the necessary operation; 2nd by performing on fresh organs, specifically on a sheep brain, any verification that would seem right to prove the physiological working of the liquids under observation.

After Aristide had formed this mental program, he only had to think about how to do it as quickly as possible. He was worried about choosing patients whose desperate condition would leave no room for doubt, but he decided on the butcher who would be responsible for delivering the fresh, healthy hearts. Then he focused on the overall approach of his opening speech.

While doing all this, he strode along the Seine not paying attention to where he was going, went up Champs Elysées and then went back down, crossed over the bridge at Invalides and went along the Left Bank.

Suddenly he noticed that he was dying of hunger and had arrived at the new station of Orléans. He went into the cafeteria. While eating he got the idea of opening up a schedule and looking at the time. And he saw that an express train from Limoges was arriving. Naturally he thought of checking to see if, by chance, Professor Falcimaigne was there.

He was there. Aristide was at the head of the platform for less than three minutes when he saw the professor get off the train and head for the exit where his car was waiting for him.

He caught up with him, told him quickly about the day's events and sat next to him to go back to l'Etoile. The professor seemed literally enchanted by the news. He had, of course, received his wife's telegrams and already felt better on his return, but he was anxious to know the details, which Aristide told him.

"I was really worried about how things would turn out," he confessed, "when I found out what my daughter had suggested. Of course, I thought that in one way or another we would manage to prove your sincerity, but we're dealing with a crafty fellow in that Bordier and without the demonstration that you're going to put against him, I really think that you won't be acquitted. I can tell you now that you should consider the matter settled! My dear boy, these are the most dangerous waters I've seen in my ship of life—and yours," he laughed. "As for your battle plan, it's well thought out and I hope that it will be decisive. But let's hold all the trumps! Don't be caught sleeping!"

The car stopped in front of the door but Aristide did not want to show up before Madame Falcimaigne so late in the evening, so he asked his teacher to give her and his daughter his most sincere thanks.

As he was leaving he saw Gertrude on the third floor balcony waiting for her father's car.

14. Battle Stations

Doctor Cordat noticed a police sergeant waiting for him at his front door.

"You weren't home," the officer said when he saw him, "and I had orders to wait to give this letter to you personally. It's from the Prefect."

He tactfully and discreetly wanted to leave after fulfilling his mission, which was easy to understand, but Aristide insisted that he come up to his apartment in case he had to give an immediate answer. He got him something to drink, showed him a chair by the fire and opened the official letter.

"Dear Doctor," the Prefect wrote, "I have seen the Public Prosecutor and he refuses to arrest you, despite your request. He thinks that you yourself should clear up the matter, as you intend to do, and leaves it to you to make the necessary arrangements. For my part I have shown to the newspapers the letter you gave me for the Prosecution and also ordered the administration at Pont Notre Dame to make the remains of the three victims available to the morticians to be transported to wherever you say. You will find attached a copy of my instructions to that effect. Very Sincerely Yours…"

Aristide right away told the sergeant about the two papers to make sure he would be conscientious about the letters he was going to give him. He wrote a quick thank you note to the Prefect and then this letter to the secretary of the Mutual Autopsy Society about his rights to the remains of Spiridon Tasimoura:

"Doctor Cordat would like to thank the official at the depot at Pont Notre Dame, on the authorization of the Prefect of Police, for delivering to the bearer of this note, the secretary of the Anthropological Society, the remains of Spiridon Tasimoura, which have been entrusted to his expertise."

"There you go, Sergeant," he gave him the two letters after rereading the one he had just received. "What I ask of you is first to make sure this letter gets to the Prefect's office first thing in the morning before taking this other to the Anthropological Society in the Dupuytren Museum at the Ecole Pratique at the end of Rue Hautefeuille. Also tell the secretary that I will visit his office before noon to talk about the list of experts who should be invited to the autopsy."

Stuffed with these instructions and a big glass of rum, the sergeant skipped out. Aristide stayed there alone to go over the details of the great battle. He was anxious to get started, but he really wanted to leave nothing to chance and to hold all the trumps, following the wise counsel of Professor Falcimaigne. He took the trouble to pick out of the phone book the names and addresses of the guests whom he figured would be the most qualified to attend the grand proof. He jotted down in a notebook not only the list of devices and accessories that he would need for his demonstration, but also the carefully thought out plan for his conference. He did not even want to think about resting until everything was all ready to the last detail. And yet, when he lay down on his bed, he fell asleep almost right away and slept like a baby so well that when the valet came with the newspapers "he had to wake up this other Alexander from a deep sleep," as the saying goes.[8]

---

[8] From Jacques-Bénigne Bossuet, Funeral Oration for Louis de Bourbon.

A quick glance assured Aristide that the Prefect had kept his word. His letter to the Public Prosecutor was everywhere, along with the Prosecution's decision and the announcement of a public experiment where everything up in the air about the matter would be explained.

Aristide had nothing to do but take a walk. He got ready and went out.

First he went to Pont Notre Dame where he saw that they were carrying out the necessary preparations. Then he went to Père Lachaise cemetery where he watched the two coffins of Pia and Antonio Baselli being placed in a temporary vault. Finally he went to the Anthropological Society.

The secretary had already seen the sergeant who brought him the letter. He eagerly made himself available to Aristide, agreeing that the proposed demonstration could take place that evening in the Society's amphitheater and he would take care of the physical preparations for it. He approved the guest list and went to a nearby lithographer who promised to deliver the invitations within two hours, which they would then send out in pneumatic envelopes.

By noon everything was ready and Aristide could go and have lunch with Professor Falcimaigne whom he naturally wanted to ask to chair the conference and to update him on the preparations. The whole household welcomed him enthusiastically and approved of all the measures taken, which he described in detail. His teacher thought it might be better to take a little more time, maybe a two- or three-day delay, but he understood better than anyone that Aristide was in a hurry to explain everything in public and was grateful for it. Moreover, at the clinic he had already been convinced of the turnaround in public opinion brought about by his ex-student's letter to the Public Prosecutor. On the evening before, all of Paris was hearing about the imminent climax; in the morning it made the rounds of all the hospitals; and by noon the press was already putting it in print. And when Aristide went back home he was flooded with requests for invitations.

It was literally impossible for him to answer all the requests because the room he had available could only hold 300 people. He could probably have chosen another venue, for example a concert hall in the afternoon. But he did not really care if nosy onlookers could satisfy their trivial curiosity. In his eyes the important thing was to speak to an elite public, a truly competent audience who could understand directly and judge his explanations with full knowledge of the facts. So, he made an announcement that he sent by telegram to all the evening papers that he was sorry but it was impossible for him to answer all the requests for invitations that he received; that he had wanted to give the explanations in court; that he was not granted this so he wanted, at least, to say everything before an audience that truly represented the French scientific community; and therefore: 1st no one would be admitted without a personal invitation presented beforehand to the secretary; 2nd the invitations sent were reserved exclusively for a limited number of professors from the Schools of Medicine and Science at the College of France and the Museum and to an equally limited number of doctors and surgeons from the hospitals in Paris, to members of the Society that was kind to him, to a very few magistrates and to a dozen reporters chosen among those who usually follow the works of the scientific community.

Instead of calming down the impatient public, this avowal only made them more angry so that in the early hours of the evening the whole population of the schools along with many other people even less qualified to deal with great scientific events went as a mob to the Dupuytren Museum. At 8 p.m. the whole area around the room, including the staircase and the hallways, was invaded by 2000 or 3000 nosy people asking for admission, which was impossible to give them. The place became impossible to get through and the guests with invitations would not have been able to get to their seats if the "devoted" secretary had not solved the problem by making them first go into the Museum where they were admitted one by one on presenting their pass and then led to the upper floors by a secret staircase that brought them into the room.

Thanks to these strategic measures, all the invitees ended up sitting down in their assigned seats within about 30 or 40 minutes and when the speaker sat down with his glass of sweet water on the table in front of him, he was in the presence of the most competent assembly that could possibly be gathered under such circumstances. At his feet was a long board on two portable stands on which the body of Spiridon rested, covered with a cloth that made him look like an Egyptian mummy. To the right and left at the back of the room Aristide recognized the familiar faces of his teachers and colleagues. In one of the first rows he saw Professor Bordier, who was one of the first he believed he had to invite. Behind him in an armchair Professor Falcimaigne opened the meeting and gave Doctor Cordat the floor.

Aristide went straight into it. In clear and simple language he put the question in its proper place. The assembly knew under what sad and tragic circumstances he was forced to answer the hasty judgments of an ignorant mob by calling upon the most qualified men to pronounce their learned opinion of a purely scientific affair in full knowledge of the facts.

A combination of trivial events without any professional interest carried the orator across the sea to the coast of Sardinia after he graduated from school. Totally out of the blue and without any forethought he entered an old Phoenician fortress that had probably been abandoned for centuries on the western coast of the island. This visit was not paid willingly or voluntarily. While he was having breakfast in the shadows of the battlements, he was attacked suddenly and thoroughly with anesthesia. After an unknown length of time he woke up on a table in an underground anatomy laboratory, strapped down under an electric light to be duly dissected. His left arm had already been prepared by exposing around a foot of the muscles with two strips of skin held back by hooks. Moreover, on the table next to him was a subject entirely emptied of his vital organs, who turned out to be (he found out later) the son of his Sardinian hosts who had been weeping and searching for him for ten days.

To support his speech Aristide quickly pulled up his left sleeve and presented it to the assembly to show the still fresh traces of the incision that he had suffered from the deltoid to the wrist. This much-needed and simply performed exhibition highlighted his speech so strongly that the whole audience, whatever their initial opinions were—and they were stamped with an icy silence—was won over at that very second and utterly convinced of his sincerity.

The speaker did not dwell on the incident. He ran through what followed: how a mute and masked person had come to finish off the work; how he had seen him delay his task to bandage him with a strange balm and plunge his patient back into anaesthetized sleep; how he woke up for a second time and got lucky, was able to cut the straps with a scalpel that was forgotten on the torture table; how he was able to get up, leave the laboratory and explore his surroundings... All this was told quickly. He told about the procession of ants that he saw working in the crypts, the wheat growing in the crypts under electric lights, the storerooms where he sated his hunger with the powerfully bracing and stimulating properties of this wheat. Then he described the gigantic staircase that led him to the grotto where his boat was waiting for him and where the three workmen were busy with the repairs.

He summarized what happened at dinner on the beach, the sudden appearance of the anatomist who had had him under his scalpel for such a long time, the two gunshots and the torturer's falling on the sandy shore. He carried him right away on board his yacht and then with the help of the reagents found in the dissection laboratory he gave him the same treatment that had produced such quick and decisive effects on himself. With this treatment Spiridon recovered from his torpor in two days and devoured the ant wheat brought up from his underground fields. He was persuaded to go to France with the victim of his scientific curiosity and of his total absence of morality (in the human sense)—but he compensated for this with a love of his race or better to say of his clan of ants whom he was the most elevated representative, the chief and absolute master. So Spiridon Tasimoura decided to follow the one who had become, in these two tragic meetings, his doctor and his friend.

Spiridon's history and family was no less extraordinary than his physique. The audience was about to verify this directly because the subject on the table, who was going to be examined first and then, if the assembly wished to appoint someone, would undergo a detailed anatomical study whose conclusions would later be summarized in a public report—this subject, lately delivered to the Mutual Autopsy Society according to a signed testament, is none other than the anatomist of the Phoenician Tower, the Emperor of the Ants, Spiridon Tasimoura, one of the unfortunate victims of the recent fire on Avenue du Bois.

While a deep silence fell over the room, Aristide Cordat went up to the table and swept away the sheet that was covering the subject.

The breathless audience saw the lifeless remains of him who had been Spiridon Tasimoura and who stood out clearly on the white sheet with his distinctive skull, his prismatic ears, his strong mandibles, his narrow thorax, his horny abdomen, his antennae and crab feet—like a huge ant developed to an extraordinary degree—but still an ant, as monstrous as it was unquestionable.

The heat from the gaslights and from the audience itself in the cramped room had thawed the subject, which appeared in its natural form, like an awkward hymenoptera, with its carapace polished black and brown, stained by the mud, shimmering under the harsh light of the lamps, which emphasized his abnormal character.

"You are asking yourselves and you will ask me, Messieurs," Aristide continued, "how I could have exchanged ideas and information with this creature who looks to you like a giant insect, like an insect lying under the lens of a microscope, but without any of the attributes of its species or its weaknesses. I'll tell you right now that it was chance, or rather the logic of circumstances, at the time when I lifted up the subject after wounding him with my rifle and checked his condition by feeling for a pulse—under my fingers I did not feel arterial pulsations but a veritable telegram from the nerves in Morse code, consisting of dots and dashes unconsciously coming through the flesh of my fingers and relaying, in Italian, a perfectly clear message."

(Shouts and exclamations, among which were clearly heard cries of disbelief). "I know, Messieurs, that such a statement might rightly astonish some of you who have done me the honor of being here! For the time being I ask you to be patient and to hear me out and not make any hasty judgments until the anatomical examination of the antennae takes place—an examination that will be entrusted to the most competent doctors, if you wish to appoint them yourselves either from the audience or from outside. This examination will prove beyond the shadow of a doubt that on the surface of the skin, on the face of the palm of said antennae there are organs appropriate for the *transmission of thought*, which I noted as Morse code in Italian. These special organs may be unfamiliar to doctors and surgeons in hospitals, but not to entomologists, especially since the work of Gryllus, Graber and Lubbock who have clearly described and shown that on the tibia of several species of ants, in particular the phridole, there are vibrating nerve sacs *that are and can only be* organs of communication, of mental perception and transmission."

"Definitely!" one of the most renowned masters of the Museum of Natural History blurted out during the pause.

"These organs," Aristide continued, "can be found on the antennae here like they can be found on the antennae of normal ants by all the specialists who have studied the subject over the last 50 years. And since this is so, Messieurs, since the organs in question are present on the palms of the antennae of this giant ant, just like on the miniature antennae of his fellow ants, why say, by what right can you say that they are useless and inactive here when they are not so among the ants in our fields and gardens? Let me say that it would be unjust and absurd! The proportions of his size, for a living being, are insignificant details. It doesn't matter, philosophically speaking, whether an ant is microscopic or gigantic! The law is constant and the organ presupposes the function, as if it created it. It would be paradoxical and absurd if it were any other way. When you find the taste buds on his tongue, you will know, beyond a doubt, that the subject could taste his food during his life. From the time when Spiridon got his vibrating nerve sacs on the palm of his antennae, it's logical and necessary that he used them to transmit his thoughts to his fellow ants or other living beings—he had to! And let me add that this communication was done and had to be done *in Italian* because Spiridon never knew another language and all his books, from his first alphabet to the manuals on anatomy that he used to dissect his subjects—all these books were in Italian, as is only natural on an Italian island!"

A round of applause cut the speaker short. But it was clear that the applause was meant for the logic of his reasoning more than for the strength of his argument. Most of the audience remained silent and attentive, reserving their approval for later.

"I'm not asking you, Messieurs," Aristide went on, "to blindly accept the explanations that I am forced to give to clear things up. I'm only asking you to accept them conditionally, as a hypothesis that is necessary for the development of the arguments that I have to present to you.

"The experts whom you yourselves will assign will say whether the subject's antennae possess the special organs that I noted. They will say whether they could be, physiologically speaking, meant for any other function.

"As for me, I simply claim that Spiridon Tasimoura, the giant ant whom you see before you, had no other way to communicate his thoughts; that this way was enough for me to unconsciously transmit thoughts from our first contact because the mental transmission was done in Italian, which I know personally from my mother who was Italian; and that this communication presented me with no difficulties.

"With this said, and you have to agree, anyway, that these preliminaries were not without some use, let me go on to what happened next. Spiridon felt confident in my care and in my general attitude to his intentions, which I, too, would have had in his place. He was quickly healed by the products that he had made and that I had, of course, brought back from his laboratory since I had experienced their power on myself. Little by little Spiridon told me (by the process I said) about his origins and his history. His race had been brought to the island by a Phoenician colony and through its travels and studies was initiated in the Chaldean traditions as well as those of ancient Egypt. For thousands of years it had been in the isolated fortress where chance brought me and where invasions, wars and revolutions have flooded through the ages without disturbing them and even without being aware of the tiny ant people who were living there peacefully. Since time immemorial these hymenoptera carried out their farming tasks by using the processes of intensive cultivation that past civilizations had shown them, defended as they were against the outside world because of their size and their isolation.

"The power of their race is entrusted to a guardian of the secrets of their society who has received them through an uninterrupted transmission from the ancestors of the high priests of India and Chaldea. The sovereignty of this chief is maintained not only by his exclusive possession of these secrets, but also by his gigantic size and superior intelligence resulting from constant and continual care that is diligently given to him from his larval state by a special upbringing reserved only for the bearer of tradition.

"You must excuse these details, which I have to explain, firstly because while Spiridon was alive I wasn't able to talk in public about the partial secrets that I gradually got out of him; and then because I wasn't able to find out more about the means he used to produce his truly miraculous operations. I still hope to discover these means by experimentation or by chance. I would have no doubt discovered them some day if Spiridon had lived because his trust in me and his broadmindedness would have come together during his contact with the outside world from which he had always been separated. His sudden death in these tragic circumstances, which would be too long to explain here in this first meeting, has cut off the progress and the hopes of this diligent collaboration with him whom I believe I can call here in our time the *last representative of the hieratic science*. This science, which is barbaric in some aspects but miraculously fruitful in some results that our science has not yet achieved—this science has to remain a ruthless mystery to us from now on since the ultimate repository, who is gone and gone forever, lies before you, a little pile of perishable ashes! Messieurs, all that's left for me to tell you in this necessarily brief explanation is the circumstance that allowed me to make a semi-public demonstration of these miraculous secrets with Spiridon Tasimoura; and also to share with you some of these secrets with the cooperation of all modern science and its most eminent representatives.

"In the first place I would like to say that Spiridon possessed a few chemical formulae whose details he did not wish to reveal to me—elixirs that were both anesthetic and fortifying and that he developed in total secrecy. I experienced these myself at his hands after having been opened and explored by his scalpel; and then on him after I shot him almost fatally as I've already told you. Both of these experiences left no doubt in my mind about the power and efficacy of the means used, even though their composition remained a mystery.

"Later in Paris, even though I didn't manage to break Spiridon's silence, I supplied him with certain chemicals and preparations on his request with written orders and I was able to persuade him to try them out on some absolutely hopeless patients in the presence of a small number of chosen witnesses.

"You are aware of how tragically Spiridon died and how his whole chemistry lab perished with him. But I'm glad to say that there was a temporary laboratory where he worked alone while our permanent house was being fixed up and it has fortunately remained intact. I found it the day before yesterday exactly as Spiridon had left it with a few bottles containing the products of his making. These products will be made available to the chemists whom you will assign to analyze, describe, verify and make public their properties!" (Shouts of approval broke out almost at the same time as unanimous and repeated applause). "That, Messieurs, will be our task. Before moving on, I would like to show you what I base my hopes on and the results we got in the first experiment before some of our dearest and most respected scholars. I plan to present one of the products Spiridon left behind in his first laboratory and to let you experience firsthand the positive effects that—from my first bandaging after the meticulous dissection—after an almost instantaneous healing—from Spiridon himself on the day after two gunshots to the head—the positive effects that give me hope and courage to attempt a new experiment on patients who are considered lost, but today will be as good as new.

"Here, Messieurs, is the product in question. I don't know the composition or the preparation. I just recognized it by its typical smell as one of the ones used on my own bandage. So, here is a perfectly healthy heart of a sheep that was killed last night and given to me by Monsieur Sauffray, a butcher on Rue Saint Honoré. I am connecting the end of the aorta to the outside tube of a Sphygmograph and with the help of this rubber bladder I'm going to make the sheep blood enter it. The sheep's blood is physiologically pure and has been preserved in a fluid state in the way you all know about. Now, for those in the audience who are not physiologists excuse me for not dwelling on the extra details, but remember that the Sphygmograph has been commonly used in our laboratories for at least 50 years; by means of the moveable drum of the cylinder it marks down the blood pressure of a living being. You see, Messieurs, that by pressing this bladder I am sending normal blood into the cavities of the heart and that the blood is causing no contraction, waking no sign of life, in a word, it is producing no more effect than pure water would, if it were still possible to get any from the taps in Paris.

"Well, Messieurs, you have observed the inactivity of the heart with the inflow of normal blood that I gave it. Now I am going to treat the same blood with a few drops of Spiridon Tasimoura's preparation. Notice the immediate effect!"

Aristide did as he said. He opened the little flask that he had taken out of his pocket and with the help of a glass eye-dropper he put a few drops into the blood leading straight to the right ventricle of the sheep's heart through a large glass tube.

Almost immediately the dead, motionless organ, the heart that had not reacted to the blood stream from the aorta *beat* strongly, kicking up its tip toward the speaker. Then it fell back down, only to beat again…then it fell down and beat again to a steady, normal, exact rhythm so that the onlookers thought they had a human heart with a strong pulse beating before their eyes.

A thunder of applause broke out, filled the room and was repeated three times on all the benches. When it was pretty much quieted down, a man stood up in the first row of the semi-circle. It was Professor Bordier. He motioned that he wanted to say something and in a clear and resonant voice he exclaimed, "I ask that the experiment be repeated in front of us on the subject we have before our eyes!"

These words fell like a shower of ice on the excitement and enthusiasm of the assembly. Everyone became quiet to wait to see what would happen. Even outside the medical field, the impact of his attacks in the "Surgical Gazette" had been formidable—to tell the truth they were a dreadful indictment against the experiments of Avenue du Bois. Everyone felt that by personally intervening in the question submitted to the audience at the very moment when the effective power of the unidentified elixir had just been triumphantly proven, the professor from Velpeau Hospital was playing his final card. In fact his situation was such that as both a theoretician and practitioner, by throwing himself openly into the fray, he had to either reduce his opponent to nothing or ruin himself beyond repair. So, they were naturally waiting impatiently for Doctor Cordat's reply when Professor Falcimaigne, as chair, stood up to make a very well-advised observation.

"It is the rule in a conference like this," he said coldly, "that the speaker alone has the floor to develop his subject. Although it may not be a universal law observed in all civilized countries not to ask a speaker in the middle of his talk to improvise on an experiment that he couldn't either foresee or prepare ahead of time, it would be, in any case, an indispensable rule in our situation where moral and even legal issues of the most serious nature are at stake.

"In reality, Doctor Cordat has put himself under the protection of the assembly here by making it a voluntary judge of a matter that is very delicate both in the moral and professional sense. He should stay in complete control of his subject. And I think that in this respect everyone will agree with me unanimously." (Yes! Yes! Of course! Repeated applause.) "Let me add that if it is still polite and fair to let a speaker choose for himself the limits of his speech, it is all the more necessary in the present case not to surprise him with a problem that is not only unreasonable but also in formal opposition to all the laws of nature, both for men and other species of animals. As Doctor Cordat told you and as each of you can see for yourself, we are in the presence of an abnormal being, a kind of monster. This abnormal being was stabbed in the eye, which made part of its brain spurt out of his left orbit, and has been dead for almost five days already. It was placed in a refrigerated room and underwent an examination by two sworn experts. No one doubts its loss of life. If it was, by its own will and according to the precise instructions of its testament, brought here to be studied anatomically, it is simple, natural and legitimate to proceed with this study. This does not mean using the remains in a useless, wild experiment that would be—let's say things as they are—trying to *resurrect* it after five days and nights as a frozen corpse. Messieurs, we are not here to perform miracles and certainly not to carry out a hoax! We are only here to listen to Doctor Cordat explain such a distressing affair and to appoint the experts to proceed firstly with the analysis of the unidentified products that have been given to us and secondly with the anatomical examination of the subject brought to us by the Mutual Autopsy Society. I propose to the assembly to keep to these two planned juries and get on with the vote!" (Movements in the audience and applause.)

Professor Bordier stood up and asked for the floor to justify his motion.

"I am sure, Messieurs, you see that I cannot accept what you've just heard without protest. In the first place, I have to flatly refuse the allegation of having thought of organizing a hoax here. I reject the term as unfair and I refer it back to the speaker! Not only am I not thinking of anything of the kind, but I honestly admit that I am truly amazed by the experiment we've just witnessed—this heart removed from its living host last night, which we've seen with our own eyes reanimate and beat. This is not a run of the mill, meaningless phenomenon! It's an innovation of the utmost importance. I think it can justify all our hopes and endeavors. And it's precisely because I'm so incredibly amazed that the idea naturally came to me—and I'm sure it came to more than one of you, too—to check if, by chance, the same effect might not be produced here on the subject that is lying on the table!" (Movements in the audience, repeated applause and shouting, "It's true! It's true! Why not?") "They told you, Messieurs, and for my part I'm completely ready to admit it after what I've just seen, that the tonic or elixir that's submitted for your examination has already produced amazing effects. The first time it brought back the use of the speaker's arm, which had undergone two successive dissections—he showed us the traces of it. The second time this unique pharmaceutical healed the brain of the subject we have before us, when this brain was shot full, and almost point-blank, with no.2 buckshot meant for big game. The third time this unidentified liquid came into play in a series of operations that I didn't see, since I didn't have the honor of being invited, but that were surely critical, seeing that it was a matter of removing an aneurysm of the aorta and from the second patient part of a lung with tuberculosis and a paralyzed optic nerve for the third. I won't talk about these facts and I accept them as proven. I just want to say one thing, Messieurs: we have been specially and personally invited here to observe the effects of a new tonic that will be examined. We have seen with our own eyes that this tonic has the amazing property of making a sheep's heart beat after it had been taken out its corporeal housing for 24 hours. Now, it happens that we have at hand the inanimate remains of the inventor or keeper of this tonic and this inventor, under previous circumstances, was proven to be responsive to the action of this liquid to the point of being able to take two shots of no.2 lead full in the head. And under these circumstances it's impossible for me not to think that it is extremely fortunate that this same inventor is lying before us today after being stabbed in the brain with a stiletto. He is dead, true, undeniably dead, but in a state of perfect preservation, for which we have to thank the thoughtful arrangements of the Paris Morgue. And by another, truly special fortune, it happens that on the speaker's table there is the liquid itself, the unidentified liquid that produced those wonderful effects and that just now revived the heart that was hooked up to the Sphygmograph.

"Messieurs, we are here, and I say this with no vanity, as the most competent judges in the world to make an observation that will be decisive. This observation can consist of trying to see if what this tonic just did on the sheep's organ can be done on the circulatory system of a giant ant that was frozen for five days and nights, but is certainly thawed out now, if I can judge by the room temperature." (Laughs and applause.) "Well, Messieurs, that's my proposition. It's simple and natural and we can do it in a few minutes—the foremost surgeons, chemists and naturalists in the world are here. There's no danger in doing this since the subject is being saved for an autopsy anyway. There's no risk of endangering the power of the elixir, which is going to be judged by its worth. It won't even change the results because we can very well admit beforehand that even if the liquid can't resurrect the dead, it doesn't necessarily follow that it can't be used to heal the living. Messieurs, I have said why the experiment seems easy to perform. I have said why it can be sure proof. Finally, allow me to state that if it's possible, it would be inhuman and almost criminal not to try it!"

Professor Bordier's reply ended in a thunder of applause and cheering. Everyone jumped up to second the motion that had just been put forward. Everyone was ready to vote.

Aristide Cordat did not hesitate for a second to go along with what would be a unanimous decision.

"Messieurs," he confessed, "for my part I see no problem with the experiment that you have proposed. I only want to take note of the fact that it was requested by Professor Bordier formally and ostensibly on the grounds that we will not, if it fails, try to use it against the former experiments. And I ask the assembly if it will be kind enough to assign the expert anatomists and chemists who will deal with the subject first so they can take full responsibility from now on. Finally, to put the seal of approval on what is going to happen, I propose that Professor Bordier be personally in charge of the operation that he recommends."

"I accept!" the spiteful surgeon from Velpeau Hospital shouted.

And the motion of the speaker was repeated by the chair and immediately voted on by the assembly. Right after that the names of all the experts were chosen and voted on by acclamation.

15. The Decisive Proof

When the preliminaries had finished, Professor Bordier changed his clothes, put on a white apron and went up to the table on which Spiridon was lying.

Tools popped up everywhere. There was no lack of volunteers to help. But there was one question that was asked right away. Should he open the chest and operate directly on one of the large arterial trunks leading to the heart? The professor hesitated and clearly stated why: he had never studied the anatomy of ants and when it came to surgery he did not like to venture into the unknown. In his view, for this species, it should be enough to isolate one of the smaller arteries in the left "arm," that is the leg or upper antenna that he had at hand and to use it to inject some of the experimental liquid directly into the circulatory system with the help of a little Pravaz device, i.e. a syringe. That way they would avoid losing value or making useless mistakes in a future autopsy. Moreover, if the liquid really had the stimulating, tonic qualities that the earlier experiments seemed to affirm, it would be unnecessary to dig around inside to any great extent.

Let's take note here that Professor Bordier was entirely in his element there on stage. He thought he was in his own amphitheater working on a difficult operation and, as was his habit because he spoke well and willingly, he could ask for nothing more than to lecture his elite audience before crossing swords.

Aristide, on the other hand, could not help noticing with pleasure that it was no longer a question of denying his previous experiments. They admitted and accepted them without a word as the basis on which they were going to work and which would have a permanent place among famous operations from now on. What seemed abominable and criminal two days earlier was now highly recommended, or at least legitimate and normal. They spoke about them as accepted, indisputable facts. They had come to the point of wishing and even secretly hoping for total success because they were joking outright about the poor subject's case.

"What's nice about this one is that we don't have to worry about putting the subject to sleep!" the professor laughed out loud. "He's stiff and unconscious enough. He's like a piece of wood covered in iron. Or horn! See these shriveled up claws, that's where we have to search for the radial artery. I honestly admit that I have no idea where it is. Do ants have only one? Ah, my father, curses on you for not having made me spend time on the anatomy of hymenoptera, as Molière would say if he were still in this world to make fun of us. Seriously, if there is a naturalist here to teach us about the particularities of ants, he is welcome at the table!"

At this call, a venerable old bald man with gold glasses got up and went up to the surgeon. At first sight he looked around 70 or 80 years old.

"Monsieur Gervaise, assistant at the Museum of Natural History," he said softly to introduce himself.

"Monsieur Gervaise!" the professor cried out in amazement. "It's your books I dug up 40 years ago when I was studying for my 'limited' degree. That's what they called it back in my day when we didn't study Greek or Latin for medical school. But how is it, Monsieur, that you are simply an assistant when your books were first rate?"

"To stay an assistant is easier than you might think," the good doctor smiled. "You only have to not push ahead when everyone else is rushing forward."

"You should be a tenured professor, at least!"

"I do my job. My boss is an old, very old student of Flourens who has taken his doctrine to heart and refuses to grow old. He thinks he's a very young man since he's not yet 103."

The students around the table started laughing. But the surgeon took advantage of the situation to find out about the state of the subject.

"No one is better qualified than the renowned author of *The Life of Ants* to give an opinion on the species of animal that we have before our eyes. In your opinion, is it really an ant?"

"Unquestionably. Anyway, it has the exterior characteristics that are extraordinarily developed overall, but clearly atrophied in certain ways. In my opinion it's an *oecodoma cephalotes major*, very major and a most beautiful specimen, with two antennae and two lower limbs systematically atrophied, a pair of upper limbs and legs that are so abnormally developed that they could be taken for human arms and legs with a little prosthetic trimming. The shape of the head, jaws, thorax and abdomen, on the other hand, remain absolutely ant-like and the brain in that strong skull under these two lateral bulges must be abnormally developed."

"Would you say for certain that you have here a gigantic ant?"

"An ant belonging to the class called *formica fusca* and the variety *oecodoma*, yes, Professor."

"I don't think this insect has any organs to speak or hear."

"It has no larynx, for sure. And it has no similar organ that could be used to emit sound. As for hearing, it's much more uncertain even though an ant is insensible to most sounds perceived by the human ear. But it could and should perceive sounds differently to us. The nerve bulges that are developed on the ends of the upper limbs where they form a kind of resonating chamber are probably real eardrums. These special organs, which are probably abnormally developed in the subject and will be very interesting to study, might very well be unable to hear the boom of a cannon, for example, but might be used to perceive underground sounds that are totally unknown to us or that we hear without listening to them.

"As for the circulation of blood, the action of the nourishing liquid on the general nutrition and especially on the respiratory organs is similar to that of man. Similar is right, but not identical! There is reason to think that it is much less active and, to a certain extent, stagnant. In the deep tissue the blood should act like a bath where the tissues will soak it up and be penetrated by the natural chemical actions. Anyway, that's how I would explain the fast, almost immediate regeneration that Doctor Cordat noted in the circumstance he just described to us when the subject got two gunshots in the head and no trace was left after two days of treatment."

"If I understand you correctly, Professor, you suppose that a similar treatment on the subject in its present condition with the same balm that has already healed so quickly could produce, under the present circumstances, the same results?"

"I would not at all be surprised, although it's not up to me to draw any positive conclusions about it. I've had many opportunities to observe ants, wasps and other insects that were horribly injured and then apparently died.

But with appropriate treatment and sometimes with an accidental change in nature—such as good weather after a rain or the sunrise after a freezing night—they showed a veritable resurrection. By this I mean a more or less absolute return to life following an apparent death. Moreover, this particularity is not exclusive to ants on land; it is found in a lot of sea life, which just has to be thrown on the dry shore to seem dead and then bathed again in its native water to come back to life.

"In conclusion, Monsieur, you figure that you will have a chance at success in trying to bring this subject here back to the light? I believe so, too. But I wouldn't be at all surprised if it had no effect."

"And, in your opinion, how should we proceed with this experiment? Do you think we should open up the thorax and go for the circulatory center?"

"That seems useless to me and could be dangerous. It would probably be enough, at least for a preliminary check, to isolate a secondary artery, the brachial or femoral, for example, and inject a very small amount of the revivifying liquid. After seeing the effect, or absence thereof, we could then decide on the next step."

"Messieurs, have you heard Monsieur Gervaise's opinion?" the professor addressed the audience who was silent during the speech. "He is surely the most qualified in all matters concerning the life and death of ants. Do you agree that we should do as he suggests and begin by isolating the brachial artery to shoot a little of this unidentified liquid? In case we notice an obvious effect, we can proceed with the usual bandaging. In the opposite case we can go straight ahead with a more direct intervention, for example, in the circulatory and nerve center."

"Yes! Yes! That's it! Start with the brachial," a number of voices bore witness to the passionate interest that everyone had in this dramatic experiment.

"Well, Messieurs, I will do as you have decided and start by looking for the brachial artery to open it up."

With these very precise instructions the professor made a large incision in the forearm of the subject. Pale, thin flesh appeared, which was nothing like the scarlet muscles of a human subject. But the operator easily found some large white vessels lying under the dermis along the length of the nerves, which Monsieur Gervaise pointed out right away as the sensory developments he had talked about—auditory organs? Or vessels to transmit nerve messages coming from the center?

No one could say for sure. The operator was still probing the muscle mass with the clamp. He ended up finding what he was looking for and with the metal tip he lifted up what was undoubtedly an arterial tube. All the expert witnesses agreed with him.

Then, using the little Pravaz syringe that Aristide Cordat held ready to give him, the operator pierced the arterial trunk, pushed in the thin, silver tube and started turning the screw that would shoot the unidentified tonic into the open artery.

When the piston reached the end of the tube, the device was filled up again. The operation was repeated three times in a row without showing any visible effects. The audience started showing signs of disappointment at the uselessness of these actions when a sudden movement appeared in the middle of the watchful group around the table.

Something like a shiver seemed to pass through the cold, still body that they were leaning over. Hands went eagerly to chosen points to search for a pulse. And right away Monsieur Gervaise, who was feeling the right arm, broke the silence with his clear voice.

"There's no doubt about it, I have a pulse!"

Professor Bordier brought his free hand straight to the place that the assistant indicated and repeated, "There's a pulse! It's unquestionable!"

They waited in silence for a few seconds.

And then suddenly the giant ant's entire body contracted like it got an electric shock and shot up from the funeral table so fast and violently that the spectators at the farthest end of the room saw it like they were standing next to it.

The auditorium was filled with a hullaballoo of shouts and whispers. The operator's assistants had their hands full trying to control the desperate jolts of the patient, who was suddenly straightened up, almost sitting, and waving around his arms wildly, breathing heavily…and finally sneezing noisily and violently.

At the same time he was opening and closing his mandibles like he was chewing, closing his claws like he was grabbing and lifting his legs like he was running.

He finally fell back down on the table and did not move, either because he was worn out or because he experienced an indefinable feeling of humiliation and anger at being the focus of so many eyes. He did not close his eyes, since he had no eyelids to do this, but grabbed the sheet and covered his face like a mask.

However, Professor Bordier took advantage of the lull to apply a cotton pad and an antiseptic bandage on the open artery. He checked that the patient's pulse was beating regularly and right away ordered his assistants to control the patient. He lifted the cloth that was masking the face and started pushing back with his fingers the hernia of cerebral matter around the right orbit.

Feeling the skilled but tyrannical hand Spiridon twisted around frantically, panting and trying relentlessly to free himself. But when everything was over and especially when he felt his ocellus covered with a compress that Aristide Cordat had just soaked with the rest of the bottle, he calmed down and stopped moving.

"Where should we take him?" asked the Secretary of the Mutual Autopsy Society who had just witnessed with deep interest, no doubt mixed with a few professional gasps, the unquestionable resurrection of the subject that he himself had brought from the Morgue seven or eight hours earlier.

"I will take him home with me," Aristide said, "but if it's possible to set up a temporary bed here, I think that would be wiser and more convenient for the immediate care that he might need. Don't you think so?" he turned to Falcimaigne and Bordier who were overcome by surprise and joy and shaking each other's hands like friends amid the unanimous applause of the witnesses of this unforgettable operation.

Two days later Spiridon was out of danger and unquestionably resurrected under the nose of the Schools and the Academies, and to the esteemed recognition of the medical journals and daily newspapers, as well as to the friends and fiercest of critics of Aristide Cordat.

But even if all disinterested men agreed in their unqualified approval and praise, both in Paris and abroad where the impact of the decisive conference had been tremendous, one man came out of it deeply disappointed by the experience, which had nevertheless exonerated him personally: it was Aristide Cordat.

In the first place, he had a hard time getting over the stunning finesse with which Professor Bordier quickly burned what he had worshipped, flaunting out loud his sudden conversion and carving out a predominant role in the victory.

On the other hand, he had no reason to congratulate himself on either the conclusions reached by the experts who were in charge of analyzing the new ant serum (as they agreed to call it) or on the convalescence of the poor giant ant who was under his watch from then on.

As for the serum, the unanimous verdict, which was signed by the experts after conflicting analyses and secret discussions that lasted for five days, was not the answer to the huge pressure of curiosity and hope that had galvanized the world for a moment.

The experts, every one of which was a renowned chemist belonging to the Academy of Sciences, the Museum, the College de France and the Sorbonne, were all in agreement on the material composition of the serum and the validity of their methods could not be doubted. But out of their theoretical agreement came a clear disagreement about the heart of the question.

The report they all signed was vague and indecisive. It began by relating in detail the different technical procedures that they had each taken in analyzing the part of the liquid given to them. Added to this information, in immense detail, was a conclusion that was so skimpy and cautious as a judgment for the whole study that they could not help noting the holes.

The document said, "In sum, the liquid submitted to our expertise should be considered as being of organic origin with a base of formic acid mixed with a vegetal element that seems to be a kind of aromatic, volatile camphor specially modified either by an animal mucus with characteristic forms noted by all the analyses or by a treatment of electricity, probably of physiological origin, that turns this plasma into a kind of liquid ozone that is extremely malleable and tonic."

"Only one point! And that's why your girl is silent!" Professor Bordier laughed loud when he had savored the diplomatic masterpiece in the evening paper that had the scoop. "Well! These chemists are easily satisfied if they imagine that they've given us a bone to chew on with this report. After reading this I know exactly as much as I did when Spiridon Tasimoura was resurrected. You have to do it over again, Messieurs, because whoever can get the real ant serum out of your paper can call himself an unqualified genius!"

Nevertheless, he did not wait to get to work on trying to reconstruct the famous serum in secret himself, which everyone was already asking him to do. And he was not the only one to chase the dream! Industrialists, chemists and amateurs alike got to work and were already yelling on page four of 20 newspapers that they had figured out the powerful formula and could henceforth breathe life back into the dead—not to speak of the simply sick.

Alone among these searchers for the philosopher's stone one man admitted that he was barely any farther along than when Spiridon's precious reserve had been found in his temporary rooms. And this man was Aristide Cordat. On the day after the memorable experience, like everyone in the medical world and no doubt many with more skill than most of his imitators, he started experimenting on the matter. He seemed to have a trump in his hand that the others lacked: Spiridon himself, who had come back from the Morgue as if to bring him the solution to the problem.

Unfortunately either Spiridon was not in the mood to explain anything or he was unable anymore.

16. Conclusion

Spiridon seemed completely healed from his terrible wound. He showed no signs of physical or moral pain, but for all that he was even more silent because neither his reason nor his memory survived the stiletto of poor Pia Baselli. His nerve center remained deeply changed. Not only was he unable to name everyday things or recall the technical ideas whose treasure had been slowly accumulated by his ancestors and had blossomed in his memory to form, so to speak, the archives of his race and the greatest heritage of vanished peoples whom it had survived...but also all of his actions, although they were not absolutely unreasonable, from then on had no connection with his memory and were extremely weak-willed.

His laboratory was of no interest to him anymore. His Italian books and journals left him indifferent. Whether at the window where he spent hours, not to say days, or in the garden on Avenue du Bois where Aristide often brought him to get some sun and try to revive some memories, he remained glum and unmoved, like a stranger to the outside world. His organs of communication—the air and nerve pockets in his forearm—where his friend had once used to feel, like searching for a pulse, the faithful translation of his thoughts and feelings—these unusual organs, which Tyndall compared to *stethoscopes*, answered no questions anymore or if they let out some unconscious message, some distant reflection of an internal or external sensation, the images remained hazy and uncertain.

Aristide tried in vain in all kinds of ways to rekindle the light gone out. Electric currents, bandages soaked in ant serum, stimulating baths, mineral waters, various tonics, one thing after another was tried without any marked effect. Current experiences were as powerless to wake him from this persistent apathy as were allusions to his past.

Only one thing, for an instant, seemed to arouse a shadow of an interest in the miserable monster who was reduced to a vegetative life: it was the company of ants who started working hard at the foot of a stone bench in the yard of Cordat's house when spring brought them out of their winter sleep.

Spiridon contemplated them, stared at their comings and goings like an old wise man for whom the various movements held no mystery.

This obvious attention ended up inspiring Doctor Cordat with an idea that he soon scolded himself for not having had right away.

A statement from the branch of the Bank of Marseille had notified him that his last precious stones had finally been sold and in the final count he still had 763,075 at his disposal. He used it right away to rebuild his house—this time with incombustible material that was especially suited for their hygienic and surgical ends: glazed brick, glass and tempered steel. The remains of the little museum recovered from the ruins made the new construction look ancient, like some kind of memory of Pompeii. The architect was the same one who had so gallantly neglected to get the insurance contracts signed and he estimated that two months of further work was necessary to finish his new masterpiece.

The interest that Spiridon had so clearly taken in the ants at the park produced in the young surgeon's mind the idea of bringing him back to Sardinia to check if the ruins of the castle might not awaken some glimmer of intelligence and memory. Professor Falcimaigne, who had worked hard with his student on trying to revive Spiridon's mind, strongly agreed with the brilliant idea. Gertrude, who had come to look upon the family friend as a big brother, was the only one who seemed opposed to the trip. She thought it was useless and even dangerous, given the huge impact that the Sardinian adventure had had in the world.

Aristide won her over by asking her to become his wife and turn the trip into a honeymoon. "At the decisive moment," he added, "you were the best and most ingenious of my helpers in the battle that I undertook against professional errors and injustice. Why not take this role on to the end by becoming my family advisor forever?"

"Why not?" Gertrude asked herself, smiling, because the proposition delighted her.

Neither the professor nor Gertrude's mother said anything against the arrangement that crowned their secret wish. And thus the matter was settled. There was no reason to drag things out too long, so three weeks later the wedding took place. Aristide had written to Napoleoni, the old sailor in Marseille who was in charge of keeping La Mouette in the harbor of the Old Port, to prepare everything for a trip to Sardinia where he would sail it if he were in the mood. The evening of the wedding he caught an express train at Gare de Lyon with the new Madame Cordat, Spiridon and a chambermaid. The next morning they all got off at the foot of La Canebière and thanks to Napoleoni's preparations everything was ready. The newlyweds and their company only had to bring their suitcases on board and give the signal for departure.

The accommodations were not elegant, but the marvelous sun over the "glassy sea" spread its humble rays on the honeymoon and when the little yacht passed the breakwater of La Joliette to head southeast, everyone on board was delighted, including Spiridon, who seemed to be vaguely conscious of the improvised departure to his fragrant island, and Gertrude, who clapped her hands in joy like a bird batting its wings. Only the maid was downcast and sad under the first effects of seasickness.

Napoleoni, however, was wondering secretly if he should be angry at going to Sardinia when he had such a beautiful boat under his feet and the right to choose his itinerary and could head for the orange trees of Ajaccio in Corsica.

But there was not a problem in the world. The breeze was good and carried the yacht on its starboard side. The weather was gentle and fresh. The seasickness was simply a menace and soon forgotten during the 20 hours of sailing. At midnight they passed Cap Corse and in the morning were in sight of La Maddalena. Before sunset La Mouette was again in its former mooring in the creek that the *castello* once so proudly towered over.

The yacht was hauled into the grotto and everyone slept peacefully. The next morning the travelers left the boat in the hands of Napoleoni and went up the monumental staircase.

At first sight nothing had changed. The volcanic explosion that the Italian cordite had caused under the castle seemed not to have shaken the gigantic stairs, but at the top it was different.

The rubble blocked up the underground room where the turbine of the electric factory once turned, but was now demolished, motionless and silent. The river still ran toward the abyss leaving the higher steps of the staircase bare and distinct among the ruins. So, the visitors climbed up the last ramp with no problem and came to the gaping hole where the crypts and wheat fields once spread out in the Phoenician palace. Not a trace remained; nor of the laboratory where Aristide had been dissected alive; nor of the incline leading to the abandoned treasure. The walls themselves, which were launched into the nearby sea by the explosion, had been ripped out of the ground like worn-out teeth and only the faint trace of their foundations was left behind.

On an isolated ridge that remained standing on the edge of the black gulf, the last trace of the Carthaginian tower, a green shrub, an offshoot of a vanished trunk, blossomed with the first buds of the year. At the bottom of the crater the grass grew thickly, blanketing the horror of the abyss. There was no way to escape the chaos caused by the explosion. There was no trace of what had been a powerful fortress. There was nothing but emptiness and nothingness.

Oppressed by this scene of death, the visitors sat down next to each other on the grass. They stayed silent, devastated by the emotion of the yawning gulf that surrounded them.

Suddenly Aristide lifted his head and saw Spiridon who seemed to be intensely curious about something at his feet in the grass. He leaned over and saw five or six ants—no more—working hard at dragging the same number of wheat grains toward a minuscule cave. He leaned farther over to see better and understood why Spiridon was so intensely interested.

These ants were survivors of the catastrophe, the "last Abencerrages" of the exterminated family that had carried in its microscopic womb the highest tradition of the Chaldeans and Medes, whose chief and erstwhile master did not even remember them.

The thought that these tiny creatures, without knowing it, held the magic power to distil the ant serum that modern science was unable to reconstruct, took hold of Aristide to the point of giving him to time to hesitate.

He searched his pockets for a box or container of some kind where he could house the precious ants. He found a box of matches, a measly box of incombustible, uninflammable Tunisian match heads. He emptied it, picked up the unconscious little creatures one by one and closed them up in the makeshift prison.

Gertrude woke up from her reverie and watched him do this.

"What are you picking up there so carefully, my dear?" she asked a little surprised.

"What am I picking up? A germ of the past that might be the future!" he said, misty-eyed, and he showed it to Spiridon who had already forgotten his little twin sisters and fallen back into the darkness of his unknown dream. "Dear, the gold bricks and gems that lay here for four or five centuries have disappeared forever with the tower, carried away by the turmoil, but our trip will not have been in vain because we will take back what could potentially be the ant serum of tomorrow. I'll tell you all about it later. For now, let's be satisfied. Our journey is not lost!"

A few months later the "last Abencerrages" were set up in the garden on Avenue du Bois at the foot of the model house. They prospered marvelously and cultivated their heroic wheat under the watchful eye of Spiridon.

Aristide is waiting patiently for them to grow enough to supply the serum and expects to open an ant dairy farm in 10 or 12 years. The latest news was that he became the father of a wonderful baby whom he named Spiridon in honor of his unfortunate friend and who might be lucky enough to succeed him as prince of the ants if his father's hopes are even half-fulfilled.

SF & FANTASY

Guy d'Armen. *Doc Ardan: The City of Gold and Lepers*
G.-J. Arnaud. *The Ice Company*
Aloysius Bertrand. *Gaspard de la Nuit*
Félix Bodin. *The Novel of the Future*
André Caroff. *The Terror of Madame Atomos*
Didier de Chousy. *Ignis*
C. I. Defontenay. *Star (Psi Cassiopeia)*
Charles Derennes. *The People of the Pole*
Harry Dickson. *The Heir of Dracula*
Jules Dornay. *Lord Ruthven Begins*
Sâr Dubnotal *vs. Jack the Ripper*
Alexandre Dumas. *The Return of Lord Ruthven*
J.-C. Dunyach. *The Night Orchid. The Thieves of Silence*
Henri Duvernois. *The Man Who Found Himself*
Henri Falk. *The Age of Lead*
Paul Féval. *Anne of the Isles. Knightshade. Revenants. Vampire City. The Vampire Countess. The Wandering Jew's Daughter*
Paul Féval, *fils*. *Felifax, the Tiger-Man*
Arnould Galopin. *Doctor Omega*
Nathalie Henneberg. *The Green Gods*
V. Hugo, Foucher & Meurice. *The Hunchback of Notre-Dame*
Michel Jeury. *Chronolysis*
O. Joncquel & Theo Varlet. *The Martian Epic*
Gérard Klein. *The Mote in Time's Eye*
Jean de La Hire. *Enter the Nyctalope. The Nyctalope on Mars. The Nyctalope vs. Lucifer*
André Laurie. *Spiridon*
G. Le Faure & H. de Graffigny. *The Extraordinary Adventures of a Russian Scientist Across the Solar System* (2 vols.)
Gustave Le Rouge. *The Vampires of Mars*
Jules Lermina. *Mysteryville. Panic in Paris. To-Ho and the Gold Destroyers*

Jean-Marc & Randy Lofficier. *Edgar Allan Poe on Mars. The Katrina Protocol. Pacifica. Robonocchio. Tales of the Shadowmen* (anthos.; 6 vols.)
Xavier Maumejean. *The League of Heroes*
John-Antoine Nau. *Enemy Force*
Marie Nizet. *Captain Vampire*
C. Nodier, Beraud & Toussaint-Merle. *Frankenstein*
Henri de Parville. *An Inhabitant of the Planet Mars*
Polidori, C. Nodier, E. Scribe. *Lord Ruthven the Vampire*
P.-A. Ponson du Terrail. *The Vampire and the Devil's Son*
Maurice Renard. *The Blue Peril. Doctor Lerne. The Doctored Man . A Man Among the Microbes. The Master of Light*
Albert Robida. *The Adventures of Saturnin Farandoul. The Clock of the Centuries.*
J.-H. Rosny Aîné. *Helgvor of the Blue River. The Givreuse Enigma. The Mysterious Force. The Navigators of Space. Vamireh. The World of the Variants. The Young Vampire*
Brian Stableford. *The New Faust at the Tragicomique. Frankenstein and the Vampire Countess. The Shadow of Frankenstein. Sherlock Holmes & The Vampires of Eternity. The Stones of Camelot. The Wayward Muse.* (anthologist) *The Germans on Venus. News from the Moon*
Jacques Spitz. *The Eye of Purgatory*
Kurt Steiner. *Ortog*
Villiers de l'Isle-Adam. *The Scaffold. The Vampire Soul*
Philippe Ward. *Artahe*
Philippe Ward & Sylvie Miller. *The Song of Montségur*

MYSTERIES & THRILLERS

M. Allain & P. Souvestre. *The Daughter of Fantômas*
Anicet-Bourgeois, Lucien Dabril. *Rocambole*
A. Bisson & G. Livet. *Nick Carter vs. Fantômas*
V. Darlay & H. de Gorsse. *Lupin vs. Holmes: The Stage Play*
Paul Féval. *Gentlemen of the Night. John Devil. The Black Coats: The Cadet Gang. The Companions of the Treasure.*

Heart of Steel. The Invisible Weapon. The Parisian Jungle. 'Salem Street
Emile Gaboriau. *Monsieur Lecoq*
Steve Leadley. *Sherlock Holmes: The Circle of Blood*
Maurice Leblanc. *Arsène Lupin vs. Countess Cagliostro. Lupin vs. Holmes: The Blonde Phantom. The Hollow Needle.*
Gaston Leroux. *Chéri-Bibi. The Phantom of the Opera. Rouletabille & the Mystery of the Yellow Room*
William Patrick Maynard. *The Terror of Fu Manchu*
Frank J. Morlock. *Sherlock Holmes: The Grand Horizontals*
P. de Wattyne & Y. Walter. *Sherlock Holmes vs. Fantômas*
David White. *Fantômas in America*

SCREENPLAYS

Mike Baron. *The Iron Triangle*
Emma Bull & Will Shetterly. *Nightspeeder. War for the Oaks*
Gerry Conway & Roy Thomas. *Doc Dynamo*
Steve Englehart. *Majorca*
James Hudnall. *The Devastator*
Jean-Marc & Randy Lofficier. *Royal Flush*
J.-M. & R. Lofficier & Marc Agapit. *Despair*
Andrew Paquette. *Peripheral Vision*
R. Thomas, J. Hendler & L. Sprague de Camp. *Rivers of Time*

NON-FICTION

Stephen R. Bissette. *Blur 1-5. Green Mountain Cinema 1*
Win Scott Eckert. *Crossovers* (2 vols.)
Jean-Marc & Randy Lofficier. *Shadowmen* (2 vols.)
Randy Lofficier. *Over Here*

HEXAGON COMICS

Franco Frescura & Luciano Bernasconi. *Wampus 1*
Franco Frescura & Giorgio Trevisan. *CLASH*
Luciano Bernasconi, Jean-Marc Lofficier & Juan Roncagliolo Berger. *Phenix 1*
Claude Legrand, Jean-Marc Lofficier & Luciano Bernasconi. *Kabur 1*
Franco Oneta. *Zembla 1*
Lina Buffolente, Jean-Marc Lofficier & Jean-Jacques Dzialowski. *Stangers 1: Homicron*
Danilo Grossi. *Strangers 2: Jaydee*
Claude Legrand & Luciano Bernasconi. *Strangers 3: Starlock*

ART BOOKS

Jean-Pierre Normand. *Science Fiction Illustrations*
Raven Okeefe. *Raven's L'il Critters*
Randy Lofficier & Raven OKeefe. *If Your Possum Go Daylight...*
Daniele Serra. *Illusions*

Milton Keynes UK
Ingram Content Group UK Ltd.
UKHW041212220324
439862UK00001B/24